"It might be about money, sweetheart."

Her chest puffed out, pushing the front of the sleeveless blouse she wore. "I am not your sweetheart. And don't think I don't remember you, Detective Krolikowski. I know you and your partner picked up my brother before he was arrested. That case is closed."

"Maybe, but your fiancé's murder isn't. And we think you and your brother know something about it."

"This is about Richard?" Her eyes widened. But when he thought she'd start that reticent eye contact thing again, she surprised him by actually taking a step closer to the edge of the porch. "Now we're finally getting to the point, aren't we? Are you accusing me again of poisoning him? So I'm a suspect, not a victim. And here I thought you'd shown up because—"

"Because what?" He pulled the toy with a noose around its neck from behind his back and watched her sink back into the chair. "You want to tell us what the hell is going on with you?"

D0362536

KANSAS CITY SECRETS

USA TODAY Bestselling Author

JULIE MILLER

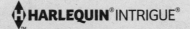
HARLEQUIN® INTRIGUE®

For my mom. It was challenging to write this book amongst unforeseen events that demanded my attention. But I wouldn't have traded your wonderful visit and recovery time for anything. I'm glad you're feeling better. I love you.

ISBN-13: 978-0-373-69849-3

Kansas City Secrets

Copyright © 2015 by Julie Miller

Recycling programs for this product may not exist in your area.

Printed in U.S.A.

Julie Miller is an award-winning *USA TODAY* bestselling author of breathtaking romantic suspense—with a National Readers' Choice Award and a Daphne du Maurier Award, among other prizes. She has also earned an *RT Book Reviews* Career Achievement Award. For a complete list of her books, monthly newsletter and more, go to juliemiller.org.

Books by Julie Miller

Harlequin Intrigue

The Precinct: Cold Case

Kansas City Cover-Up
Kansas City Secrets

The Precinct

Beauty and the Badge
Takedown
KCPD Protector
Crossfire Christmas

The Precinct: Task Force

The Marine Next Door
Kansas City Cowboy
Tactical Advantage
Assumed Identity
Task Force Bride
Yuletide Protector

Visit the Author Profile page at
Harlequin.com for more titles.

CAST OF CHARACTERS

Max Krolikowski—The brash, tough-talking former army sergeant now works as a Kansas City Cold Case detective. His assignment: solve a six-year-old murder by getting close to the prime suspect. But is Rosie March really a murderer? Or is the vulnerable woman with the soft gray eyes the one witness who can finally solve his case?

Rosemary "Rosie" March—This shy, dutiful woman has been the neighborhood pariah ever since she was accused of murdering her abusive fiancé, Richard Bratcher. Are the threats she's receiving because of money? Or because someone thinks she got away with murder six years ago?

Howard Bratcher—Rosemary's attorney. There was no love lost between him and his late brother.

Otis and Arlene Dinkle—Are Rosie's neighbors protective or nosy?

Charleen Grimes—One of Richard's mistresses. She doesn't mince words about who she thinks killed her lover.

Leland Asher—The mob boss might be in prison, but he still has connections in Kansas City. Is someone continuing to carry out his orders?

Dr. Hillary Wells—The CEO of Endicott Global. Her company produced the drug that killed Richard Bratcher.

Hudson Kramer—A new detective at KCPD with an eye for the ladies.

Stephen March—Rosie's brother is in prison. The best way to ensure his silence is to threaten his sister.

Richard Bratcher—The victim of an unsolved murder that KCPD's Cold Case Squad is working on. Few people mourn his passing, though. Especially since his evil seems to reach right out of the grave to wreak havoc on the lives he touched.

The Host—The one person who seems to know the truth about several of KCPD's Cold Case murders.

Chapter One

"Why did you kill that woman, Stephen?" Rosemary March asked, looking across the scarred-up table at her younger brother. "And don't tell me it was to rob her for drug money. I know that isn't who you are."

Rosemary studied the twenty-eight-year-old man she'd done her best to raise after a small plane crash several years earlier had left them orphans. She tried to pretend there weren't a dozen pairs of eyes on her, watching through the observation windows around them. It was easier than pretending the Missouri State Penitentiary's tiny visitation room with its locked steel doors wasn't making her claustrophobic.

But it was impossible to ignore the clinking of the chains and cuffs that bound Stephen March's wrists and ankles together. "You ask me that every time you come to see me, Rosemary."

"Because I'm not satisfied with the answers you've given me." She ran her fingers beneath the collar of her floral-print blouse, telling herself it was the heat of the Missouri summer, and not any discomfiting leer from another prisoner or the unsettling mystery of why her brother would kill a woman he didn't know, that made beads of perspiration gather against her skin. "I hate seeing you in here."

"You need to let it go. This is where I deserve to be. Trust me, sis. I was never going to amount to much on the outside."

"That's not true. With your artistic talent you could have—"

"But I didn't." He drummed his scarred fingers together at the edge of the table. For as long as she'd known him, he'd been hyper like that—always moving, always full of energy. Their father had gotten him into running cross-country and track; their mother had put a drawing pencil in his hand. Ultimately, though, neither outlet could compete with the meth addiction that had sent his life spiraling out of control. "Losing Mom and Dad was no excuse for me going off the deep end and not helping out. Especially when your fiancé…" The drumming stopped abruptly. "Just know, I was really there for you when you needed me."

"Needed you for what? If you had anything to do with Richard's murder, please tell me. You know I'll forgive you. We never used to keep secrets like this from each other. Please help me understand."

"I kept you safe. That's the one thing I got right, the one thing I'm proud of. Even the Colonel would have finally been proud of me," he added, referring to their father.

"Dad loved you," Rosemary insisted.

"Maybe. But he wasn't real thrilled having a drug addict for a son, was he? But I took action. The way he would have." His gaze darted around the room, as if checking for eavesdroppers, before his light brown eyes focused on her and he dropped his voice to a whisper. "For the last time, I killed that lady reporter to protect you."

Understanding far more about tragedy and violence

and not being able to protect herself and her loved ones more than she'd ever wanted to, Rosemary brushed aside the escaping wisps of her copper-red hair and leaned forward, pressing the argument. "Dad wouldn't have wanted you to commit murder. I didn't even know that woman. That's what doesn't make any sense. What kind of threat was she to me?"

Stephen groaned at her repeated demands for a straightforward explanation. He slumped back in his chair and nodded toward the family's current attorney standing outside the window behind her. "Why did you bring him?"

Fine. She'd let him change the topic. Although it was good to see Stephen clean and sober, he looked exhausted. Her younger brother had aged considerably in the months since he'd pleaded guilty to second-degree murder and been incarcerated, and she didn't want to add to his stress. She glanced over her shoulder to the brown-haired man in the suit and tie and returned his smile before facing her brother again. "Howard insisted on coming with me. He didn't want me driving back to Kansas City at night by myself. It was a kind offer."

The drumming started again. "He reminds me too much of his brother. Are you sure he's treating you right?"

She flinched at the remembered shock of Richard Bratcher's open hand across her mouth putting an end to an argument they'd had over a memorial scholarship she'd wanted to set up in her parents' names. Seven years later, she could still taste the metallic tang of blood in her mouth that reminded her she'd made a colossal mistake in inviting the attorney into their lives, falling in love with him, trusting him. Rosemary inhaled a quiet breath and lifted her chin. Richard was dead and she'd become a pro at setting aside those horrible memories and pasting a facade of cool serenity on her face.

"They may look alike, but Howard isn't like his brother. Howard's never laid a hand on me. In fact, I think he feels so guilty about how Richard treated us when I was engaged to him that he goes out of his way to be helpful."

"He's just keeping you close so you won't sue his law firm."

"Maybe." Initially, she'd been leery of Howard's offer to take over as the family's attorney. But he knew more than anyone else about the wrongful death and injury suit Richard Bratcher had filed against the aerospace manufacturer that built the faulty plane her father had flown on that fateful trip, and she couldn't stand to drag the suit out any longer than it had already lasted. Plus, he'd been nothing but a gentleman and rock-solid support through the continuing upheavals in her life. "Howard makes it easier to get in to see you. And he's responsible for keeping you in the infirmary wing to do your rehab instead of you being sent back to general lockup with the other prisoners."

"Don't stick with him because of me. I can handle myself in here. I don't trust him, sis."

Rosemary's smile became genuine. "You don't trust anybody."

Stephen sat up straight and reached for her. At the last second, he remembered the guard at door and raised both hands to show they were empty. Rosemary held up her hands, as well, and got a nod of approval before reaching over the battered tabletop to hold her brother's hands. "I trust you. I'm okay being in here because I know you're safe now. You *are* safe, right?"

Stephen's grip tightened, as if somehow sensing that

all was not well in her life. But Rosemary clenched her jaw and continued to smile. The last thing he needed was to worry about her on the outside, when he couldn't do a thing about it. "I am."

She was right now, at any rate.

The assurance seemed to ease his concern. He eased his grip but didn't let go. "That bastard Richard is dead. But it'd kill me if I thought his brother or anyone else was hurting you."

"I'm fine." What were a few obscene phone calls, anyway, after all they'd been through? Her hope had been to find a few answers for herself, not raise doubts in her brother's mind. "As much as we both wanted Richard out of our lives, I know you didn't kill him." Stephen had been in a rehab facility in the middle of a forty-eight-hour lockdown the morning she'd discovered her fiancé dead in bed at his condo, poisoned sometime during the night. She, however, had had no alibi and had spent several months as KCPD's number one suspect until the trail of clues went cold and Richard Bratcher's murder had been relegated to the cold-case files. Rosemary squeezed her brother's hands. "Whoever poisoned him did us a favor. But if you're protecting someone who wanted that reporter dead, or you're taking the blame for her murder because you wished you'd been the one to kill Richard… Please, Stephen. Talk to me."

His eyes darkened for a split second before he shook his head and pulled away. "I was using that night. I pulled the trigger. Now I'm done talking about it. You should be, too."

"Why?"

"Rosemary—" He bit down on a curse and folded his hands together, his finger tracing the marks he'd left in his own skin back in the days when he'd been too stressed-out to cope or on a manic high.

"It's okay, Stephen," she quickly assured him, alarmed by the frantic, self-destructive habit he'd worked so hard to overcome. "I won't mention it again."

This visit, at any rate.

Reluctantly, she acquiesced to his demand and sat back in her chair. She knew there had to be more to Stephen's motive for killing an innocent reporter than simply being high as a kite and not knowing what he was doing, as he'd stated in court. The monster in their own home had been the real threat, and, in her heart, she believed there was a connection between the two murders—a logical reason her brother was going to spend half his adult life in prison and she was going to be alone. But if Stephen wouldn't talk, she wasn't certain how else she could get to the truth about the two murders and finally put the nightmares of the past behind her.

Yet, until that revelation, Rosemary stuck to the role she'd learned to play so well, dutifully taking care of others. "Is there anything you need? I brought the books you asked for, and two cartons of cigarettes." She curled her fingers into a fist, fighting the instinctive urge to reach for the neckline of her dress and the scars underneath. Instead, she arched an eyebrow in teasing reprimand. "I wish you'd give those up. You know they're not good for you."

That earned her half a grin from her brother. "Let me kick one addiction at a time, okay?"

"Okay." A high sign from the guard warned her their time was nearly up. Rosemary blinked back the tears that made her eyes gritty and smiled for Stephen's sake as he stood and waited for the guard to escort him back to his cell. "I wish I could give you a hug."

"Me, too." But that kind of contact wasn't allowed. "I love you, sis. Stay strong."

As if she had any choice. She fought to keep her smile fixed in place. "I love you. I'll keep writing. And it wouldn't hurt you to pick up a pencil every now and then, either. Be safe."

He nodded as he shuffled to the door in front of the guard. "You, too."

Rosemary was alone for only a few seconds before another guard came to the door to walk her out to the visitors' desk. But it was long enough for the smile to fade, her shoulders to sag and her heart to grow heavy. How was one woman supposed to endure so much and still keep going on with her life? She followed the rules. She'd done everything that was expected of her and more. Why wasn't it good enough? Why wasn't *she* good enough?

"Ma'am?"

With a quick swipe at the hot moisture in her eyes, Rosemary nodded and got up to accompany the guard out that door into an antechamber and then out the next one into the visitors' waiting area. She jumped at the slam of each heavy door behind her, which closed her off farther from the only family she had left. With every slam, her shoulders straightened, her heart locked up and she braced herself to meet the concern that etched frown lines beside Howard Bratcher's eyes when he greeted her. "How are you holding up?"

"I'm fine."

While she waited in line to retrieve the purse she'd checked in at the front desk, Rosemary became aware of other eyes watching her. Not quite the lecherous leer she'd imagined tracking her from the shadows each night she got one of those creepy phone calls. Certainly not the solicitous concern in Howard's hazel eyes.

When the holes boring into her back became too much to ignore, she turned.

"Rosemary?"

But she didn't see Howard standing beside her. She looked beyond him to the rows of chairs near the far wall. The girlfriends, wives and mothers waiting to see their loved ones barely acknowledged her curiosity as her gaze swept down the line. There were a couple of men in T-shirts and jeans. A few more in dress slacks and polo shirts or wearing a jacket and tie like Howard. They were reading papers, chatting with their neighbors, using their phones.

But no one was watching.

No one was interested in her at all.

She was just a skittish, paranoid woman afraid of her own shadow these days.

Hating that any sense of self-confidence and security had once again been stolen from her, she turned back to the guard at the front desk and grabbed her purse. "Thank you."

But when she fell into step beside Howard and headed toward the main doors, the hackles beneath her bun went on alert again. She was suddenly aware of the young-ish man sitting at the end of the row against the wall. He wore a loose tie at the front of the linen jacket that remained curiously unwrinkled, and he was texting on his phone.

Was it that guy? Had he been following her move-ments with that more than casual curiosity she'd felt? Although it was hard to tell if he was making eye contact through the glasses he wore, he seemed to be holding his phone at an oddly upright angle, tapping the screen. He lifted his attention from his work and briefly smiled at her before returning to whatever he found so fascinating on the tiny screen.

Like an image of her?

"Rosemary?" She felt Howard's touch at her elbow and quickly shifted her gaze back to the door he held open for her. "Is something wrong?"

"I don't know." Stepping outside, the wall of heat and humidity momentarily robbed her of breath. But her suspicion lingered. "Did you see that guy?"

"What guy?"

They were halfway across the parking lot now. "The one who was staring at me?"

Howard glanced over his shoulder and shrugged. "They probably don't see a lot of pretty women here."

Pretty? Rosemary groaned inwardly at the sly compliment. She caught a few frizzy waves that curled against her neck and tucked them into the bun at the back of her head. After Richard's abuse, the last thing she wanted was to attract a man's attention. But the curiosity of that man in the waiting room had felt like something different. She shuddered in the heat as she waited for Howard to open the door of his car for her. "I think he took a picture of me with his phone."

"So you don't mean one of the prisoners?"

"No. He was one of the attorney-looking guys out in the waiting area."

"Attorney-looking?" Howard laughed as he closed the door behind her and walked around to his side of the car. He shed his suit jacket and tossed it into the backseat before getting in. "So we're a type?"

"Sorry. I didn't mean anything negative by that. I was just describing him. Suit. Tie. Maybe more on the ball than some of the others waiting to visit friends and family here. He looked like an educated professional."

"No offense taken." He pushed the button, and the engine of the luxury car hummed to life. "Could be a reporter, getting the scoop on Kansas City's newest millionaire visiting the state penitentiary."

Right, as if hearing her picture might be in the paper again was a whole lot better than thinking someone was spying on her. "I wish you wouldn't say that."

He pushed another button to turn on the air-conditioning. "What do you want me to call it? Your brother's in the state pen. It's public record."

"No. 'Kansas City's newest millionaire.'" She supposed the soap opera of her life made her recent wealth big news in a summer where most of the local stories seemed to be about the weather. "I'd give anything if that headline had never hit the papers. I hate being the center of attention."

"Yet you handle it all with grace and decorum." Howard reached for her hand across the seat, but Rosemary pulled away before he made contact, busying herself with buckling up and adjusting the air-conditioning vents. Even as the evening hour approached, the temperature across Missouri was still in the nineties. Seeking relief from the heat was as legitimate an excuse to avoid his touch as her innate aversion to letting a man who looked so much like his late younger brother—or maybe any man, at all—get that close to her again.

With a sigh he made no effort to mask, Howard settled back behind the wheel and pulled out onto the road leading away from the prison. "Hungry for an early dinner? My treat. Jefferson City's got this great new restaurant on top of one of the hotels downtown. You can see the Capitol Building and almost all the riverfront. Day or night, it's a spectacular view."

The answering rumble in her stomach negated the

easy excuse to say she wasn't hungry. Instead, she opted for an honest compromise. "Dinner would be great. But, could we just drive through and eat it in the car? I need to get home and let the dogs out. And we still have a two-and-a-half-hour drive to Kansas City ahead of us."

Howard had seen the wrongful death and manufacturer's negligence lawsuit his brother had started for her through to its conclusion. And though she'd trade the 9.2-million-dollar settlement for her parents in a heartbeat, she was grateful to the Bratcher, Austin & Cole law firm that they'd gotten the company to admit its guilt in their construction of the faulty wing struts on the small airplane that had crashed, killing her parents instantly.

And though Howard's interest might have as much to do with the generous percentage his firm had received from the settlement, Rosemary appreciated his attempts to be kind. However, her gratitude didn't go so far as to want to encourage a more personal connection between them. She'd thought Richard Bratcher was her hero, rescuing her from the dutiful drudgery of her life, and she'd fallen hard and fast. Richard had been her first love…and her biggest mistake—one she never intended to make again. But her business relationship and friendship with his older brother, Howard, shouldn't suffer because of it. She glanced across the seat and smiled. "Is that okay?"

Knowing her history with his brother, Howard was probably relieved she hadn't given him a flat-out no. He nodded his agreement, willing, once again, to please her. "Fast food, it is."

Almost three hours later, Howard pulled off the interstate and turned toward her home on the eastern edge of Kansas City. Although it was nearly eight o'clock, the sun was still a rosy orange ball in the western sky when he walked her up onto the front porch that ran clear across the front of her ninety-year-old bungalow.

From the moment the car doors had shut and she'd stepped out, she could hear the high and low pitches of her two dogs barking, and was eager to get inside to see them. She had her keys out and her purse looped over her shoulder when she realized Howard had followed her to the top of the stairs, waiting to take his leave or maybe hoping to be invited in for coffee.

What one woman might see as polite, Rosemary saw as suffocating, maybe even dangerous. As much as she loathed going out in public, she hated the idea of being trapped inside the house with a man even more. No way was she reliving that nightmare. With the dogs scratching at the other side of the door now, anxious for her arrival, Rosemary turned and lifted her gaze to Howard's patient expression. "Thank you for going with me to Jefferson City."

"My pleasure."

"Do I owe you some gas money?"

He chuckled. "Not a penny."

Finally getting the hint that this was goodbye, he leaned in to kiss her cheek. But Rosemary extended her hand instead, forcing some space between them. "Good night, Howard."

He gently took her hand and raised it to his lips to kiss the back of her knuckles instead. "Good night. I'll pick you up tomorrow?" he asked, releasing her from the gallant gesture and pulling away.

Right. More papers to sign. "I can drive, you know."

"But the drive will give me a chance to explain the trust fund and scholarship you'll be setting up before you sign anything." There'd already been plenty of explanation and she'd made her decisions.

"Howard—"

"That way you won't have to spend any longer than a few minutes at the office."

Now *that* was a selling point. Rosemary nodded her acquiescence. "I'll be ready. See you then."

She waited until he was backing out of the driveway and waved before turning around to unlock the door. She typed in the security code to release the alarm, but her hand stopped with her key in the lock. She wasn't alone.

Was *he* watching her? Would there be another vile message waiting on her answering machine?

I see you, Rosemary. Thinking your money can buy you security. Thinking those dogs will keep you safe. One of these days it'll be just you and me. I'll show you how justice is done. I'll take you apart piece by piece.

With her shaking hand still on the key, she glanced up and down the street at the peaceful normalcy of a summer evening in the older suburban neighborhood. There was an impromptu ball game in the Johannesens' front yard across the street. Mrs. Keith was out trimming her shrubs while her husband washed the car in their driveway.

Squinting against the reflection of the sunset in her next-door neighbors' living room window, Rosemary caught the shadowy silhouette of Otis or Arlene Dinkle. The brief ripple of alarm that had put her on guard a moment earlier eased. The Dinkles had lived next door for years, and had been friends with her parents long before Rosemary had moved back home to care for her teenage brother.

Unable to get a good look at which of the couple was eyeing her, Rosemary exhaled a sigh of relief and waved. They'd watched over her for a long time, including that night Richard had attacked her and she'd run to their house to call the police, fearing he'd come back after he'd stormed out. Her wave must have been all the reassurance the Dinkles needed to know she'd arrived home safely. The shadow disappeared and the blinds closed.

Breathing easier now, Rosemary unlocked the door and went inside. "Hey, ladies. Mama's home."

Her smile was genuine as she locked the door behind her and dropped to her knees to accept the enthusiastic greeting from the German shepherd with the excited whine and the miniature poodle leaping up and down around her.

"Hey, Duchess. Hey, Trixie. I missed you guys, too." She spared a few moments to rub their tummies and accept some eager licks before rising to her feet and doing a quick walk through the house with the dogs trailing behind her.

She really should have no worries about an intruder, especially with the yappy apricot poodle and the former K-9 Corps dog who'd been dismissed from the program because of an eye injury on hand to guard the place. If the dogs weren't alarmed, she shouldn't be, either. Still, she checked all the rooms, including the guest suite upstairs, before she set her purse down beside the answering machine on the kitchen counter.

No blinking red light.

"Thank goodness."

Her day had already been long and troubling enough without having to deal with another message from the unwanted admirer she'd picked up the night after news of her settlement being finalized had appeared in the *Kansas City Journal*. And she was certain the police department was tired of her calling in to report the disturbing calls. She knew she was tired of hearing the subtle changes in their tone once she identified herself. The officers were sympathetic when they saw her name in the system as a victim of domestic violence, but seemed to think she was some kind of crank caller when they read her abuser was dead and that she had once been a suspect in his murder. They probably thought she was some sort of paranoid crazy lady—or a woman desperately seeking attention when, in reality, she'd be far more content to fade into the woodwork.

The advice from the officer she'd finally been connected with had been to keep a log of the calls and let her know if she thought they were escalating into something more serious. If she'd known when Richard Bratcher's controlling demands were going to escalate into violence, she might have been spared a split lip, a broken arm and... She ran her fingers beneath the collar of her blouse, resting her palm over the old scars there. Talk about a sudden and unexpected escalation. But when images from that horrific time tried to surface, Rosemary pulled her hand away and stooped down to busy her fingers and brain with the much more enjoyable task of petting the dogs and rubbing their bellies.

After a happy competition for her affection, Rosemary kicked off her sandals and relished the cool tile under her toes. With both dogs dancing around her, she unbolted the back door and opened the screen door to let them out into the fenced-in yard to run around.

The warm breeze wrapped her eyelet skirt around her knees and caught the wispy curls escaping from her bun and stuck them to the warm skin of her cheeks and neck. With the nubby concrete of the patio still warm beneath her feet, she glanced up at the sky and tried to gauge how long they had before nightfall. While Trixie sniffed the perimeter of the yard and the big German shepherd loped along behind her little buddy, Rosemary walked to the edge of her in-ground pool and dipped her toes into the water. As tempting as it might be to cool off in the pool, she hated to be out after dark. Besides, Duchess and Trixie had been on their own for most of the day and deserved a little one-on-one attention. A few games of fetch and tug-of-war before bedtime would do just as much to help her forget these restless urges to prod the truth from her brother, rail against the fear and loneliness that plagued nearly every waking moment and live her life like a normal person again.

Laughing as Duchess barked at a rabbit in the Dinkles' backyard garden, startling Trixie with her deep woof and setting off a not-to-be-messed-with barking from the smaller dog, Rosemary opened the storage unit at the edge of the patio where she kept pool and outdoor pet supplies. One of the shelves was dedicated to a sack of birdseed, grooming brushes and a stash of dog toys.

She pulled out the tennis ball Duchess loved to chase and gave it a good toss, watching the dogs trip over each other in their eagerness to retrieve the faded yellow orb. Then she reached inside for one of Trixie's squeaky toys and gasped.

The last rays of sunlight hitting the nape of her neck could have been shards of wintry ice as she snatched her hand away from the gruesome display inside.

"I don't understand why this is happening," she whispered through her tight throat.

But she couldn't pull her eyes away from the tiny stuffed animal—tan and curly coated like her sweet little Trixie—hanging from a noose fashioned out of twine from the cabinet's top shelf. Nor could she ignore the typed message pinned to the polyester material.

I know what you did.

You don't deserve to be rewarded.

You can't escape justice.

Who would…? Why would…?

Duchess dropped the slobbery ball at her feet, and the dogs buffeted her back and forth, eager for her to throw it again. When she didn't immediately respond, the German shepherd rose up on her hind legs to help herself to another toy inside the cabinet, and Rosemary snapped out of her shock.

"Down, girl. Get down." Rosemary pushed the black-and-tan dog aside and closed the cabinet doors. Then she latched onto Duchess's collar and swung her gaze around the yard.

Was someone watching her right now? Was some sicko out there getting off on just how terrified he could make her feel?

She led the dogs to the side gate with her to check the front of the house. No doubt picking up on her alarm, Trixie barked at nothing in particular. At least, nothing Rosemary could make out. She saw regular, light evening traffic out on the street, with all the cars driving slowly past because of the kids playing nearby. The Keiths had gone inside. There was no visible movement in the Dinkle house next door.

Rosemary's breath burned in her throat. This had gone beyond excusing those calls as some drunk who'd read her name in the paper. Somebody wanted her scared? He'd succeeded.

"Duchess, heel. Trixie?" The German shepherd fell into step beside Rosemary as she scooped up the poodle. "No one's going to hurt you, baby."

She checked the separate entrance that led to the

basement apartment where Stephen had lived when he'd gotten older. Good. Bolted tight. Then she took the dogs inside the kitchen and locked both the screen and steel doors behind her before punching in the code to reset the alarm. She flipped on the patio light, gave the dogs each her own rawhide chew and walked straight through to the front door, turning on every light inside and out.

Verifying for a second time that every room of the house was empty, Rosemary returned to the kitchen to brew a pot of green tea and fill a glass of ice to pour it over.

Her hands were shaking too hard to hold on to the frosty glass by the time she'd curled up on the library sofa with the dogs at her feet and the lights blazing. She should turn on the TV, read a book, sort through another box of papers and family mementos that had become her summer project, or get ready for bed and pretend she had any shot at sleeping now.

Rosemary deliberated each option for several moments before springing to her feet and circling around behind the large walnut desk that had been her father's. She opened the bottom drawer and pushed aside a box of photographs to unlock her father's old Army pistol from its metal box. It had been years since he'd taken her and Stephen target shooting out at a cousin's farm in the country, so she couldn't even be sure the thing still worked, much less remember exactly how to clean and load it. Still, it offered some measure of protection besides Duchess and Trixie. She pulled out the gun, magazine and a box of bullets and set them on top of the desk.

Then, even if they thought she was some sad, lonely spinster desperate for attention, she took a long swallow of her iced tea, picked up the phone and called KCPD to report the latest threat.

Chapter Two

Detective Max Krolikowski was a soldier by training. He was mission oriented. Dinkin' around on a wild-goose chase to see if some woman had talked to some guy about a crime that had occurred ages ago, just in case somebody somewhere could shed some new light on the unsolved case he and his partner from KCPD's Cold Case Squad were investigating, was not his idea of a good time.

Especially not today.

Max stepped on the accelerator of his '72 Chevy Chevelle, fisting his hand around the steering wheel in an effort to squeeze out the images of bits and pieces of fallen comrades in a remote desert village. He fought off the more troubling memory of prying a pistol out of a good man's dead hand.

He should be in a bar someplace getting drunk, or at Mount Washington Cemetery, allowing himself to weep over the grave of Army Captain James Stecher. Max and his team had rescued Jimmy from the insurgents' camp where he and two other NCOs been held hostage and tortured for seven days, but a part of Jimmy had never truly made it home. Eight years ago today, he'd put his gun in his mouth and ended the nightmares and survivor's guilt that had haunted him since their homecoming.

Max had found the body, left the Army and gone back to school to become a cop all within a year. Getting bad guys off the streets went a ways toward making his world right again. Following up on some remote, random possibility of a lead on the anniversary of Jimmy's senseless suicide did not.

"Whoa, brother." The voice of his partner, Trent Dixon, sitting in the passenger seat across from him, thankfully interrupted his dark thoughts. "We're not on a high-speed chase here. Slow it down before some uniform pulls us over."

Max rolled his eyes behind his wraparound sunglasses but lifted his foot. A little. He snickered around the unlit cigar clenched between his teeth. "Tell me again why we're drivin' out to visit this whack job Rosie March? She's hardly a reliable witness. Murder suspects generally aren't."

Tall, Dark and Hard to Rile chuckled. "Because her brother—a convicted killer with motive for killing Richard Bratcher—is our best lead to solving Bratcher's murder, and he's not talking to us. But he is talking to his sister. At least, she's the only person who visits him regularly. Maybe we can get her to tell us what he knows. Besides, you know one of the best ways to investigate a cold case like this one is to reinterview anyone associated with the original investigation. Rosemary March had motive for wanting her abusive boyfriend dead and has no alibi for the time of the murder. She'd be any smart detective's first call on this investigation. It's called doing our job."

Max shook his head at the annoyingly sensible explanation. "I had to ask."

Trent laughed outright. "Maybe you'd better let me do the talking when we get to the March house. Somehow, I doubt that calling her a *whack job* will encourage her to share any inside information she or her brother might have on our case."

"I get it. I'm the eyes and the muscle, and you're the pretty boy front man." Max plucked the cigar from his lips as he pulled off the highway on the eastern edge of Kansas City. "I'm not in the mood to make nice with some shriveled old prune of a woman, anyway."

"Rosemary March is thirty-three years old. We've got her driver's license photo in our records, and it looks as normal as any DMV pic can. What logic are you basing this I'd-rather-date-my-sister description on?"

Max could quote the file on their person of interest, too. "Over the years she's called in as many false alarms to 9-1-1 as she has legit actionable offenses, which makes her a flake in my book. Trespassing. Vandalism. Harassing phone calls. Either she's got a thing for cops, she has some kind of paranoia complex or it's the only way she can get any attention. Whatever her deal is, I'm not in the mood to play games today."

"Some of those calls were legit," Trent pointed out. "What about the abusive fiancé?"

"Our murder victim?"

"Yeah. Those complaints against Bratcher were substantiated. Even though someone scrubbed the photos and domestic violence complaints from his file after his death, the medical reports of Miss March's broken arm, bruises and other injuries were included as part of the initial murder investigation."

"But the woman's never married. She's only had the one boyfriend we can verify." Okay, so a fiancé who'd hurt her qualified as low-life devil scum, not boyfriend, in his book. But Rosemary March had money. A lot of it. Even if she had three warts on the end of her nose and looked like a gorilla, there should be a dozen men hitting on her. She should be on the social register donating to charities. She should be traveling the world or building a mansion or driving a luxury car or doing something that would make her show up on somebody's radar in Kansas City. "The woman's practically a recluse. She has her groceries delivered. She's got a teaching degree, but hasn't worked in a school since that plane wreck her parents were in. She's probably a hoarder. Her idea of a social outing is visiting her brother in prison. If that doesn't smack of crazy cat lady, I don't know what does."

"It's a wonder you've never been able to keep a woman."

Max forced a laugh, although the sound fell flat on his eardrums. Somehow, subjecting a good woman to his mood swings and bullheaded indifference to most social graces didn't seem very fair. But there were times, like today, when he regretted not having the sweet smells of a woman and the soft warmth of a welcoming body to lose himself in. Looked as though another long run or hour of lifting weights in the gym tonight would be his only escape from the sorrows of the day. "I make no claims on being a catch."

"Good, 'cause you'd lose that bet."

He wasn't the only cop in this car with relationship issues. "Give it a rest, junior. I don't see you asking me to stand up as best man anytime soon. When are you going to quit making goo-goo eyes at Katie Rinaldi and ask her out?"

"There's her son to consider. There's too much history between us." Trent muttered one of Max's favorite curses. "It's complicated."

"Women usually are."

This time, the laughter between them was genuine.

When Max and Trent both got assigned to the Cold Case Squad, their superior officer must have paired the two of them together as some kind of yin and yang thing—blond, brunette; older, younger; a veteran of a hard knocks life and an optimistic young man who'd grown up in a suburban neighborhood much like this one, with a mom and a dad and 2.5 siblings or whatever the average was these days; an enlisted soldier who'd gone into the Army right out of high school and a football-scholarship winner who'd graduated cum laude and skipped a career in the pros because of one concussion too many. Max and Trent were a textbook example of the good cop/bad cop metaphor.

And no one had ever asked Max to play the good-cop role.

But their strengths balanced each other. He had survival instincts honed on the field of battle and in the dark shadows of city streets. He was one of the few detectives in KCPD with marksman status who wasn't on a SWAT team. And if it was mechanical, he could probably get it started or keep it running with little more than the toolbox in his trunk. As for their weaknesses? Hell, Detective Goody Two-shoes over there probably didn't have any weakness. Trent wasn't just an athlete. He was book smart. Patient. Always two or three steps ahead of anybody else in the room. He was the only cop in the department who'd ever taken Max down in hand-to-hand combat training—and that was because of some brainiac trick he'd used against him. And he was one of the few people left on the planet Max trusted without question. Trent Dixon reminded Max of a certain captain he'd served under during his Army stint in the Middle East. He would have followed Jimmy Stecher to the ends of the earth and back, and, in some ways, he had.

Only Jimmy had never made it back from that last door-to-door skirmish where he and the others had been taken prisoner. Not really. Oh, Max had led the rescue and they'd shipped home on the evac plane together after that last do-or-die firefight to get him out of that desert village. They'd been in Walter Reed hospital for a few weeks together, too. The two men he'd been captured with had been shot to death in front of him. Jimmy hadn't cracked and revealed troop positions or battle strategies, and he'd never let them film him reading their latest manifesto to use him as propaganda. But part of Jimmy had died inside on that nightmarish campaign— the part that could survive in the real, normal world. And Max should have seen it coming. He'd been responsible for retrieving their dead and getting their commander out of there. But he hadn't saved Jimmy. Not really. He hadn't realized there was one more soldier who'd still needed him.

He'd failed his mission. His friend was dead.

Despite the bright summer sunshine burning through the windshield of his classic car, Max felt the darkness creeping into his thoughts. The image of what a bullet to the brain could do to a man's head was tattooed on his memories as surely as the ink marking his left shoulder. He'd known today would be a tough one—the anniversary of Jimmy's suicide.

Trent knew it, too.

"Stay with me, brother." His partner's deeply pitched voice echoed through the car, drawing Max out of his annual funk. "Not everybody's the enemy today. I need you focused on this interview."

Max nodded, slamming the door on his ugly past. He rolled the unlit cigar between his fingers and chomped down on it again. "This is busywork, and you know it."

Probably why Trent had volunteered the two of them to make this trip to the suburbs instead of sitting in the precinct office reading through files with the other detectives on the team. Max didn't blame him. Teaming with him, especially on days like this, was probably a pretty thankless job. He should be glad Trent was looking out for him. He *was* glad. Still didn't make this trip to the March house any less of a wild-goose chase when he was more in the mood to do something concrete like make an arrest or run down a perp. "Rosemary March isn't about to confess or tell us anything her brother said. If she knows something about Bratcher's murder, she's kept quiet for six years. Don't know why she'd start gettin' chatty about it now."

Trent relaxed back in his seat, maybe assured that Max was with him in the here and now. "I think she's worth checking out. Other than her brother's attorney, she's the only person who visits Stephen March down in Jeff City. If he's going to confide anything to anyone, it'll be to his sister."

"What's he gonna confide that'll do our case any good?" Max stepped on the accelerator to zip through a yellow light and turn into the suburban neighborhood. Hearing the engine hum with the power he relished beneath the hood, he pulled off his sunglasses and rubbed the dashboard. "That's my girl."

"I swear you talk sweeter to this car than any woman I've ever seen you with," Trent teased. "But seriously, we aren't running a race."

"Beats pokin' along in your pickup truck."

Besides, today of all days, he needed to be driving the Chevelle. The car had been a junker when Jimmy had bequeathed it to him. Now it was a testament to his lost commander, a link to the past, a reminder of the better man Max should have been. Restoring this car that had once belonged to Jimmy wasn't just a hobby. It was therapy for the long, lonely nights and empty days when the job and a couple of beers weren't enough to keep the memories at bay. Or when he just needed some time to think.

Right now, though, he needed to stop *thinking* and get on with the job at hand.

Max put the sunglasses back on his face and cruised another block before plucking the cigar from his lips. "Just because the team is working on some theory that this cold-case murder is related to the death of the reporter Stephen March killed, it doesn't mean they are. We've got no facts to back up the idea that March had anything to do with Bratcher's death. March used a gun. Bratcher was poisoned. March's victim was doing a story on Leland Asher and his criminal organization, and there's no evidence that Richard Bratcher was connected to Asher or the reporter. And Stephen March sure isn't part of any organized crime setup. If Liv and Lieutenant Rafferty-Taylor want to connect the two murders, I think we ought to be digging into Asher and his cronies. The mob could have any number of reasons to want to eliminate a lawyer."

"But poison?" Trent shrugged his massive shoulders. "That hardly sounds like a mob-style hit to me."

"What if Asher hired a hit *lady*? Women are more likely to kill someone using poison than a man is. And dead is dead." Max tapped his fingers with the cigar on the console between them to emphasize his point. "Facts make a case. We should be investigating any women associated with Asher and his business dealings."

But Trent was big enough and stubborn enough not to be intimidated by Max's grousing. "Even if she turns out to be a *shriveled old prune*, Rosemary March is a woman. Therefore, she meets your criteria as a potential suspect. Doesn't sound like such a wild-goose chase now, does it?"

Growling a curse at Trent's dead-on, smart-aleck logic, Max stuffed the cigar back between his teeth. It was a habit he'd picked up during his stint in the Army before college and joining the police force. And though the docs at Walter Reed had convinced him to quit lighting up so his body could heal and he could stay in fighting shape, it was a tension-relieving habit he had no intention of denying himself. Especially on stressful days like this one.

Feeling a touch of the melancholy rage that sometimes fueled his moods, Max shut down the memories that tried to creep in and nudged the accelerator to zip through another yellow light.

"You know…" Trent started, "you take better care of this car than you do yourself. Maybe you ought to re-think your priorities."

"And maybe you ought to mind your own business."

"You're my partner. You are my business."

Max glanced over at his dark-haired nemesis. Conversations like this made him feel like Trent's pop or Dutch uncle, as if life had aged him far beyond the twelve years that separated them in age. Still, Trent was the closest thing he had to a friend here in KC. The younger detective dealt with his moods and attitude better than anybody since Jimmy. Nope. He wasn't going there.

"Bite me, junior." Max pulled up to the curb in front of the white house with blue shutters and red rosebushes blooming along the front of the porch.

"I know today is a rough one for you." Trent pulled his notebook from beneath the seat before he clapped a hand on Max's shoulder. "But seriously, brother. Did you get that shirt out of the laundry? You know you're supposed to fold them or hang them up when you take them out of the dryer, right? Did you even shave this morning?"

"You are not my mama." Although part of him appreciated the concern behind Trent's teasing, Max shrugged his hand away and killed the engine. "Get out of my car. And don't scratch anything on your way out."

Max set his cigar in the ashtray and checked the rearview mirror, scrubbing his fingers over the gold-and-tan stubble that he probably should have attended to before leaving for work this morning. Although the crew cut was the same as it had been back in basic training, the wrinkled chambray of his short-sleeved shirt would have earned him a demerit and a lecture from Jimmy. What a mess. One beer too many and a sketchy night's sleep had left him ill-equipped to deal with today.

Swearing at the demons staring back at him, Max climbed out, tucking in the tails of his shirt and adjusting the badge and gun at the waist of his jeans as he surveyed up and down the street. Looked like a pretty ordinary summer morning here in middle-class America. Dogs barking out back. Flowers blooming. Kids playing in the yard. Royals baseball banners flying proudly. Didn't look like the hoity-toity neighborhood where he expected a millionaire crackpot to live. Didn't look much like a place where they could track down clues to a six-year-old murder, either.

But he had to give Trent credit for dragging him out on this fool's errand. Driving the Chevy and breathing in the fresh air beat being cooped up in the office with a bunch of paperwork and his gloomy thoughts. Max tipped his face to the sunshine for a few moments, locking down the bad memories before he took the steps two at a time and followed Trent up to the Marches' front porch.

"What is this? Fort Knox?" he drawled, eyeing the high-tech gadgetry of the alarm on the front door, along with the knob lock and dead bolt. "My grandma lives in a brand-new apartment complex and doesn't have this kind of security."

"The woman does live alone," Trent reminded him.

Max peered in through the front bay window while Trent rang the doorbell. The front room was neat as a pin, if stacks of boxes and piles of papers on nearly every flat surface counted. But not a cat in sight. He refused to believe that the noise of dogs barking out back might in any way disprove his theory about crazy Rosemary March.

"Yes?" Several seconds passed before the red steel door opened halfway. He could barely hear the woman's soft voice through the glass storm door. "May I help you?"

Trent flashed his badge and identified them. "KCPD, ma'am. I'm Detective Dixon and this is my partner, Max Krolikowski. We're here to ask some questions. Are you Rosemary March?" She must have nodded. "Could you open the outside door, too?"

"If you step back, I will. I'll disable the alarm and come out."

Max moved to one side while Trent retreated to the requested distance between them.

Max had expected that shriveled-up prune from his imagination to appear. He at least expected to see a homely plain Jane with pop-bottle glasses. He wasn't expecting the generously built woman with flawless alabaster skin, dressed neck to knee in a gauzy white dress, exposing only her arms and calves to the summer heat. Although her hair, the color of a shiny copper penny, was drawn back into a bun so tight that words like *spinster* and *schoolmarm* danced on his tongue, he hadn't expected Rosemary March to be so…feminine. So curvy. He wasn't expecting to see signs of pretty.

He wasn't expecting the Colt automatic she held down in the folds of her skirt, either.

Chapter Three

Max's fingers immediately went to his holster. "Gun!"

The redhead nudged open the glass storm door and slipped the pistol behind her back as though they wouldn't notice it. "I asked you to step—"

"Damn it, lady. Keep that thing where we can see it." Max put up one hand to swing the door open wide and folded the other hand around her arm, sliding it down over her wrist until he had the barrel of her weapon in his grasp.

"Get out of my house—" The redhead gasped and recoiled, tugging against his grip. "Let go of me."

No way. Even if she didn't mean them any harm, he wasn't trusting that a fruitcake like her wouldn't accidentally fire off a round. "Damn it, lady, relax. We're just here to talk."

She curled both hands around the butt of the weapon now. If her finger reached that trigger… "Please don't swear like that. It isn't polite."

"And pointing a gun at us is?" Two of her hands against one of his was no contest. She stumbled out the door, uselessly trying to hold on while he pried the weapon from her grip. A rush that was more anger than relief fired through his veins when he realized how light it was. "Oh, hell, no." He turned aside, dropping the empty magazine from the handle and opening the firing chamber. "This thing isn't even loaded."

Her gaze was as icy cool as her skin. "May I please have it back?"

Max turned the gun over in his hands. "This thing is Army issue. About twenty years old." He reset the magazine and thrust the Colt back at her, butt first. If she recoiled half a step at his abrupt action and loud voice, he didn't care. "It isn't yours."

"It was my father's."

"Didn't he ever tell you that you damn sure never point an empty weapon at a guy whose gun can really shoot? Hell, what if I'd pulled my sidearm instead of grabbing yours?"

Her eyes were the silvery color of twilight as she angled them up to him, searching for the intent behind his mirrored glasses. She finally took the gun from him and hugged it near her waist. "You're swearing again."

"Looking down the barrel of a gun does that to me."

"I didn't point it at you," she snapped. "You had no reason to—" And then she inhaled a calming breath and turned to Trent, as though raising her voice to Max violated some code of conduct she wouldn't allow. "I was putting away my father's pistol when the doorbell rang. If I had known you were the police, I would have locked it up first. But I thought it was my friend here to give me a ride into the city, and he would understand. He knows I don't keep it loaded."

Jimmy's hand had held an Army pistol that fateful day, too. Max's mind went hazy for a split second as the gruesome image tried to take hold. But he ruthlessly shoved it aside. Of all the stupid, fool stunts for this woman to pull today. "You don't carry a gun around unless you're prepared to use it."

"And you don't just grab a person because you—" Her chin jerked up to give him a straight-on look at the pink stains dotting her pale cheeks before she clamped her mouth shut and dropped her gaze. Well, what do you know? Crazy Dog Lady had a temper.

"Ease up, Max," Trent warned.

Those gray eyes flashed in Max's direction although she turned her body toward his partner, rightly suspecting that Trent would be the one more apt to listen to a reasonable explanation. "You should have called first. I have an appointment this morning with my attorney. I wasn't expecting anyone else to come to the house."

"Maybe we should start this conversation again." Trent raised his notebook between them and intervened, leaving Max wondering if it was his partner's presence or some snobby code of behavior that made her check her tongue when she clearly wanted to lambaste him for putting his hands on her. She turned her full focus on the taller man, dismissing Max. Trent pulled off his sunglasses and tucked them into his chest pocket. "I apologize for my partner here. His PR skills might be a little rusty, but believe me, he's a good cop. You're perfectly safe with him. There's no one else I trust to have my back more. Are you Rosemary March?"

"You already know that or you wouldn't be here."

Trent managed to keep the patient tone Max hadn't been able to muster. "First of all, is everything all right, ma'am? It tends to put us on alert to see someone carrying a weapon. I assure you, Max was only trying to prevent an accident from happening."

Her gaze darted up to his. "Is that true?"

Max shrugged. "I don't like to get shot."

"But that's why you touched me? You thought I was

going to...?" Her voice trailed away and her focus dropped to the middle of his chest. "Sarcasm, right?"

"Oh, yeah." With a clear lack of appreciation for his cynical humor, her gaze bounced across the width of Max's shoulders, up to the scruff on his chin, over to the large bay window and finally down to the brass badge clipped to his belt. Prim and proper Miss Rosemary March was hiding something, buying herself time to come up with the right thing to say. Why? Something had her spooked. Was it the badge? His very real, very loaded gun? Was it him? Six feet, two inches of growly first sergeant in need of a shave could be intimidating. Was it Trent? Max's partner was even taller, still built like the defensive lineman he'd once been. And she had to be, what, all of five-five?

A chill pricked the back of his neck. That instant wariness, much like the split-second warnings he'd gotten over in the desert before all hell broke loose, put him on alert. Maybe he and Trent weren't the reason she was carrying that gun. Thinking he ought to be worried about more than that empty weapon, Max rested his hand on his holster and looked beyond her into the foyer. "Is someone in the house with you?"

"No." Too fast an answer.

When he reached for the door, she sidestepped to block his path. She put her hand up to stop him from opening the door. Max put on the brakes, but with his momentum he swayed toward her, breathing in a whiff of her flowery soap or shampoo. He heard her suck in her breath and felt her fingers push against him before she curled them into a fist and pulled back almost as soon as they made contact with his chest.

"Lady, I'm trying to help—"

"I said no." Although the firm tone drew him up

short, the warning was directed to the button on the wrinkled point of his collar.

And she was shivering. In this ninety-degree heat, he could see the fine tremors in the fist clutched to her chest.

Max huffed out a frustrated breath that she turned her face from. He scrubbed his hand over the stubble on his jaw and wisely backed away before he muttered the curse on the tip of his tongue. He wasn't able to read this chick at all. She wasn't wrinkled. She wasn't old. And the only thing prunish about her was the snooty tone that attempted to put him in his place time and again. And, hell, he had to admire anyone who dared to stand up to him on a day like today.

First, she'd been an imposition on his time. Then she was a threat. Now he could smell the fear on her, but she refused to admit to it.

And how could he still feel the imprint of five fingers that had barely brushed against him?

He splayed his hands at his waist and demanded that she start making some sense. "Are you hiding something? Is that why you don't want us inside?"

"No, I just don't like having anyone…" She pressed her pink lips together in a thin line, stopping that explanation. "It's a mess."

The boxes and piles of papers stacked in the room indicated she was telling the truth. Still, there was something off about this woman—about this whole situation. "Nobody comes to the door with a gun because she's embarrassed about her housekeeping. That thing is an accident waiting to happen."

"I'll explain it again." Oh, right. In case the dumb cop couldn't figure it out. "The gun was still out from last night. I've been going through my parents' things for months now and found it in my father's desk. I was putting it away before my ride comes to pick me up this morning. The doorbell rang while I was straightening up. I thought it was my attorney. I didn't want to keep him waiting." Despite the even, articulate tone, her soft gray eyes kept glancing up to him but wouldn't lock on to his questioning gaze. Probably because he wasn't letting her see it. She drifted a step closer to Trent. "I wasn't expecting anyone to come to the house. The officer took a report over the phone last night. I thought someone would come over then. But no one ever did so I assumed KCPD had dismissed my call."

Huh? That comment short-circuited his fuming suspicions. Max traded a look with Trent before asking, "What report?"

"The one I called the police about last night." Last night? He'd missed something here. Had she gone back to making spurious calls to 9-1-1? While Max was wondering if his communication skills had gone completely off the rails, Rosemary March's body language changed. Her free hand went to the stand-up collar of her dress and she puffed up like a banty hen trying to assert herself in the barnyard pecking order. "Would you mind taking off your sunglasses, Detective Krolikowski? It's rude not to let someone see your eyes when you're having a conversation with them."

"What?"

"Take off your glasses. I insist."

"You insist?" Max bristled at her bossy tone. "Boy, you've got to have everything just so, don't you."

"I don't think common courtesy is asking too much."

"Max." Trent nodded at him to do it.

Really? Max pulled off his glasses and hooked them on the back of his neck. She wanted the glasses off?

How about this, honey? He folded his arms across his chest and glared down into her searching gray eyes until they suddenly shuttered. She must have had her fill of cynicism and impatience because she retreated until her back was pressed against the glass door.

He didn't need to hear the breathy tone of her polite thank-you to recognize the sudden change in Miss Rosie's demeanor or feel like a heel knowing he was the cause of it. What had he done? Most people got in his face or blew him off when he got in a mood like this. But Rosemary March was different. So what if this conversation wasn't making any sense to him. He knew better than to let anybody's odd behavior get under his skin. His presence here clearly agitated her. She breathed harder, faster, and Max topped off his jackassery by noticing her full, round breasts pushing against the gauzy white cotton of that dress.

That little seed of attraction he hadn't expected to feel was clearly agitating him. "Ah, hell. Ma'am, I didn't mean… I wish I could explain where my head is today, but it's too long a story. Are you sure you're okay?"

She nodded, but he'd feel a lot less like a scary bastard if she'd get some color in those pale cheeks or lecture him again. Putting his hand on her and crowding her probably hadn't been the smartest moves. Something about the gun must have drummed up memories of Jimmy and put him on his worst behavior.

But that was a lousy excuse for a man sworn to protect and serve. This was about more than a soldier's or a cop's hardwired reaction to giving anybody a chance to get the drop on him or his men. And he could hardly explain his skepticism regarding her usefulness as a witness on this anniversary of Jimmy's senseless death.

He owed her some kind of apology for scaring her. For being a jerk. But the words weren't coming. Not today.

When had words ever been his strong suit?

Thank God, he was part of a team and could rely on Trent's handsome face and friendly smile to salvage this interview. Max cleared his throat and backed toward the front steps. "I'll, uh, just do a quick walk around the place if that's okay with you."

Miss Rosemary gave him a jerky nod, her gaze breezing past his chin again. "I left the message in the cabinet on my patio out back." Message? Trent glanced over his shoulder and traded a confused look, but Max wasn't about to ask. "The dogs will bark, but they don't bite." And then her twilight gaze landed on his. A fine, coppery brow arched in what might be arrogance. Or a warning. "At least, they haven't bitten anyone yet."

Nope. Didn't have to hit him over the head more than once. He had no business trying to make nice with anybody today.

"I'll look." He nodded to Trent. "You talk."

Max trotted down the steps and breathed a lungful of humid summer air into his tight chest while he made another cursory scan of the well-kept front yard. When he realized the lady of the house wasn't answering any of Trent's questions with him still in sight, he muttered a curse and followed the driveway around the side of the house.

Message in a cabinet? Was that code for something? Like *Scram, Krolikowski*? And that thing about the dogs not biting anyone *yet*—was that an attempt at humor to ease the friction between them, or her demure version of a threat?

He peeked through the window of the separate garage to see her sedan parked inside, along with a neatly arranged array of storage boxes and lawn equipment. She was right about the dogs barking. As soon as he came into view, a deep-voiced German shepherd with a cloudy eye and a yappy little bundle of curly tan hair charged the chain-link fence and let him know they knew he was there.

A fond memory of Jax, the big German shepherd who'd served with his unit, made him smile. Jax had died in that Sector Six firefight where the captain had been captured. The victim of a hidden bomb. A single bark had given them their only warning before the blast. Jimmy had taken the dog's death as hard as the loss of his men. "Son of a..."

Really? Just like that, whatever positives he could summon today crashed and burned. Irritated with his inability to focus, Max fixed the friendliest look he could manage on his face and approached the fence.

"Hey, big girl. Do you sit? Sit. Good girl." When the shepherd instantly obeyed his command, he figured the poodle was the one he had to win over. He squatted down and held his fist against the chain-link fence to let the excited little dog sniff his hand. They certainly hadn't had a feisty little fuzz mop like this one with the unit. "Hey, there, killer."

When the poodle finally stopped dancing around long enough to lick his knuckles, Max figured it was safe to open the gate and go inside. Apparently, Rosie March had spent a bit of her newly acquired wealth on more than security. Though this was by no means a mansion, the old house had plenty of room for one woman, and was well taken care of. New roof and shutters. Freshly painted siding and trim. The pool in the middle of her backyard was long and narrow, meant for swimming laps instead of sunbathing beside. Yet there was still plenty of green space for the dogs to roam. He shrugged and petted the pooches, who were leading as much as following him on his stroll around the yard. Nothing looked out of place here, but then his real purpose for volunteering to do recon was so the lady of the house would take the panic level down a few notches and talk to Trent.

And he could get his head together and remember he was a cop. He needed to do better. So far, the only thing he knew for sure about this investigation was that Rosie March smelled like summer and her hesitant touch stayed with him like a brand against his skin.

Max rubbed at the spot on his chest. So what did that mean? He was lonesome enough or horny enough to think he was attracted to Miss Prim & Proper just because she'd touched him? Or was that a stamp of guilt because his big, brusque attitude had frightened the woman when he should have been calming her?

"Idiot!" Max punched the palm of his hand.

The German shepherd barked at the harsh reprimand and darted several paces away. "Easy, girl." He held out his hand and let the big dog cautiously sniff and make friends again. "I'm not mad at you. I'll bet your mama never raises her voice like that, does she." He cupped a palmful of warm fur and scratched around the dog's ears. Who was he to call Rosie the Redhead crazy? He wasn't exactly firing on all cylinders himself today. "Don't you be afraid of me, too."

While the shepherd forgave his harsh tone and pushed her head into the stroke of his hand, the poodle rolled on her back in the grass, completely comfortable with his presence there. Max chuckled. "At least somebody around here likes me."

And then he became aware of eyes on him. Not a shy

gray gaze worried about what uncouth thing he'd say or do next. But spying eyes. Suspicious eyes.

With his senses on alert, Max knelt down between the two dogs and wrestled with them both, giving himself a chance to locate the source of the curious perusal. There. East fence, hiding behind a stand of sweet corn and tomato plants. Nosy neighbor at nine o'clock. With a clap of his hands, the dogs barked and took off running at the new game.

Max pushed to his feet and zeroed in on the dark-haired woman wearing a white bandanna and gardening gloves. "Morning, ma'am."

Her eyes rounded as though startled to be discovered, and she tightened her grip on the spool of twine she'd been using to tie up the heavy-laden tomato plants. "Good morning. Are you the police?"

"Yes, ma'am." He tapped his badge on his belt. "Detective Krolikowski, KCPD. And you are…?"

"Arlene Dinkle. We've lived here going on thirty years now," she announced. "There's not going to be trouble with Rosemary again, is there?"

Again? The dogs returned and circled around his legs. Max sent them on their way again. "Trouble?"

Mrs. Dinkle parted the cornstalks that were as tall as she was and came to the fence. She lowered her voice to a conspiratorial tone. "There was a man who used to stay with her sometimes. Don't think the whole neighborhood didn't notice. Things haven't been right at this house for a long time."

Maybe he could pick up some useful information on this recon mission, after all—and make up for the interview he'd botched out on the front porch. Max strolled to the fence to join her. "You mean Miss March's fiancé? He stayed here?"

."A couple of times a week. When he was alive." The older woman clucked her tongue behind her teeth. "Some folks think she killed him, you know. Between those rumors and her juvenile delinquent brother, she definitely brought down the quality of this neighborhood."

That shy, spooked lady on the front porch brought down the neighborhood? That delicate, feminine facade could be the perfect cover for darker secrets. And if Bratcher had been here on a regular basis, she'd have had plenty of opportunity to slip him the poison that had killed him.

But he was having a hard time aligning the image of a calculated murderess with the skittish redhead who protected herself with an unloaded gun. She wasn't that good of an actress, was she? "You know anything about that murder?"

"I should say not." Unlike Rosemary March, Max could read this woman with his eyes closed. Arlene Dinkle liked to gossip. Although he found her holier-than-thou tone a little irritating, the cop in him was inclined to let her. Judging by the streaks of silver in her black hair, she'd been sticking her nose into other people's business for a long time. "Now there's all that publicity with that legal settlement or wherever her nine million dollars came from. Did you know there were reporters at her house two months ago? One of them even came to our home to find out what we knew about her."

"And you told this reporter about Miss March entertaining her fiancé overnight, what, six, seven, years ago? Did you ever see any indication that Mr. Bratcher was violent with Rosie?"

"Rosie? Oh. You mean Rosemary. Yes, there was that one time she came to our house to use our phone—said her lawyer friend who was getting her all that money after her parents' plane crash—oh, the Colonel and Meg were such good people—I don't understand how their children could turn out so—"

"What did Rosie say about her lawyer friend?" Max cut her off before she rambled away on a useless tangent.

She snorted a laugh that scraped against his eardrums. "*Rosemary* said he'd trapped her inside the house until she agreed to sign some prenuptial agreement and marry him. Made no sense at all. They were already engaged. She pounded on our door in the middle of the night, woke Otis and me both out of a sound sleep. Blubbering about how we needed to call the police." The dogs were circling again. Disapproval seeped into Arlene's tone and she pulled back from the fence. "That's when she got the big dog. Washed out of K-9 training. But I swear that dog would still take a bite out of you if you look at her crosswise. The little one digs in the topsoil of my garden, too. Reaches right under the fence. Rosemary ought to put up a privacy fence. She certainly can afford to do it."

Really? Then how would you spy on her? Max kept his sarcasm to himself and followed up on the one key word that might actually prove useful in an investigation. "You said *trapped*. Was Rosie—Miss March— injured in any way that night? Did you believe her when she told you that her fiancé hurt her? Threatened her?"

"Oh, she had some blood on her blouse and she was cradling her arm. I thought maybe she'd been in a car accident or had fallen down the stairs. We let her use the phone right away, of course, and sat with her until the ambulance and police arrived. But we saw her fiancé drive away, so I wondered why she just wouldn't use her own phone."

"If Bratcher hurt her, she was probably afraid he'd come back. Getting out of the house would be a smart survival tactic."

Arlene straightened, as though insulted that he would doubt her word against Rosie's. "Richard Bratcher was an upstanding member of the community. Why on earth a handsome, charming man like that would ever have to resort to anything so—"

"Arlene." Max caught a glimpse of movement at the sliding glass door on the Dinkles' patio before another man's voice interrupted the tale. "I'm sure the detective isn't here to chat with you. You let him be."

Arlene whirled around on the man with salt-and-pepper hair who must be her husband. "He asked me questions. We were having a conversation."

"Uh-huh." The lanky older man extended his hand over the fence. "I'm Otis Dinkle. We've lived next door to Rosemary and her family since she was a little girl. Is everything okay?"

At least Arlene had the grace to look a little ashamed that she hadn't asked that. Max lightly clasped the older man's hand, assuming that his presence meant he wasn't getting any more facts or nonsense from his wife. "Max Krolikowski, KCPD. I'm not sure, sir. My partner and I are looking into an old case." Maybe this was as good a time as any to test the veracity of Rosie's claims about receiving threats. "But I understand there may have been a disturbance here yesterday?"

"You mean like a break-in?"

Max nodded. "Or a trespasser on the property?"

"Not that I've seen." Otis tucked his fingers into the pockets of his Bermuda shorts and shrugged. "She was gone all day yesterday. I didn't see any activity after she took the dogs out for their morning walk."

"Her new attorney dropped her off last night," Arlene added. "Her dead fiancé's brother. I knew there was something funny going on. The two of them probably—"

Otis put up a hand, silencing his wife's opinion. "She didn't even let him into the house, Arlene. I don't think it's anything serious."

Max arched a curious brow. So the gossipy missus wasn't the only one watching the March house. "You saw her come home last night?"

Otis nodded. "We keep an eye on each other's place. Maybe chat in the front yard or across the fence when we're both out mowing. Other than that, though, Rosemary keeps pretty much to herself. We used to do stuff with her parents, but now that they're gone, she's just not that social."

"You didn't see anyone lurking around the house who shouldn't be?"

"Her dogs would have raised a ruckus. I didn't hear anything like that."

"They were locked up inside, Otis," Arlene reminded him.

"So, no intruders?" Max clarified. "Nothing you saw that seemed…off to you?"

Otis scratched at his bald spot, considering the question. "No, sir. Other than she didn't go for her regular swim this morning. It's been pretty quiet around here since her brother got put in jail. But then, we're retired. We don't keep late hours."

Yet he spied over the fence often enough to know Rosie's morning routine and when she came home at night. Curious.

"Well, if you do see anything suspicious, give us a

call, would you?" Max reached into his back pocket and handed the man a business card with his contact information.

Arlene clutched the ball of twine against her chest. "Are we in any danger?"

"I don't think so, ma'am."

Otis held the card out at arm's length and read it. "I'll be. Cold Case Squad? This isn't about a break-in. Are you investigating her fiancé's murder, Detective Kro-likowski? You think she did it?"

If poison wasn't such a premeditated means of murder, he might have been willing to dismiss his suspicions about Rosie as a justified case of self-defense. "Do you?"

"If you'd said Stephen, yes—that kid always was the rebellious sort. Good thing he was in rehab that week or you cops would have come down really hard on him. But honestly, I can't see Rosemary raising a hand to anybody. But what do I know? Like I said, she keeps to herself." He winked as a grin spread across his face. "It's those quiet ones you can't trust, right?"

With Arlene's snort of derisive agreement, Max reached down to pet the German shepherd, dismissing the Dinkles. He'd stomached about all he could of polite conversation today. "Remember to give me a call if you see or hear anything suspicious."

"Will do."

Max clapped his hands and played one more game of try-to-catch-me with the dogs while the couple went back to their back porch, arguing about people breaking in next door and whether or not the neighborhood was safe anymore. As he watched the two dogs run a wide circle around the perimeter of the yard, Max shook his head. If the Dinkles were his neighbors, he'd probably avoid socializing, too.

So what, exactly, would make a healthy woman of means isolate herself the way Rosie March had? Keeping a low profile was generally rule number one for someone who'd committed a crime. Was it the publicity surrounding the lawsuit and sudden fortune she'd won? There were probably friends and family coming out of the woodwork, trying to get a piece of that nine million dollars. He'd hate that kind of spotlight, too. Was she ashamed because her brother had killed a woman, robbing her for a fix? Nobody knew better than him what it felt like to miss the signs of a loved one spiraling out of control. Or was Miss Rosie March just plain ol' afraid of her own shadow because life had dealt her a raw hand? That could explain the frequent 9-1-1 calls and why she'd unpack her daddy's Army pistol.

Max had a feeling there were a whole lot of secrets that woman was keeping. Ferreting them out would require a degree of insight and patience he lacked. KCPD had better send out someone else from the team, like Olivia Watson, so they could talk woman to woman, or cool and unflappable Jim Parker, or even nice guy Trent—without his bad-cop partner tagging along to make a mess of things.

Max watched the Dinkles settle into patio chairs, shaking his head as Otis plugged in earbuds while Arlene peeled off her gloves and prattled on about too many cops and dogs and reporters for her liking. Max tuned her out, too, and whistled for the dogs to return. "Come here, girls!"

He finally conceded that this outing hadn't been a total waste of his time. He'd done some decent police work, confirming that Rosie had a motive for killing Richard Bratcher. Although Arlene had dismissed the violent details that had soured Max's stomach, a woman who'd been held hostage by her abuser might feel she had no other way out of the relationship than to murder the man who terrorized her.

He liked the dogs, too. As much as the dogs he'd served with overseas had detected bombs and alerted his unit to insurgents sneaking past the camp perimeter or lying in wait out on a patrol, they'd been the unofficial morale officers. There was little that a game of fetch or a furry body snuggled up in the bunk beside him couldn't take his mind off of for a few minutes, at least.

The muscles in his face relaxed with an unfamiliar smile as the shepherd and poodle charged toward him. But the dogs ran right past, abandoning the game. Abandoning him.

Tension gripped him again, just as quickly as it had ebbed, when he heard the clanking of the gate opening behind him. The mutts were showing their true allegiance to their copper-haired mistress by trotting up to greet her. Rosemary March followed Trent through the gate and latched it behind her, stopping on the opposite edge of the narrow pool. She knelt down in that starchy dress to accept the enthusiastic welcome of her pets, and Max's cranky, used-up heart did a funny little flip-flop at the unexpected sight of that uptight, upper-crust woman getting licked in the face and not complaining one whit about muddy, grass-stained paws on her white dress.

Great. That was the last thing he needed today, thinking he had the hots for the most viable suspect in their murder investigation—a good girl, no less, who seemed to push every bad-behavior button in his arsenal, a woman who was all kinds of wrong for him and his crass, worldly ways. She was a suspect, not an opportunity. He needed to get his head back in the game.

"Miss March was visiting her brother yesterday," Trent began, giving Max a heads-up nod across the narrow width of the pool, indicating that he'd gotten her to open up to him. Max raised a surrendering hand, promising to watch his mouth and not blow any progress Trent had made in his absence, and started a slow stroll around the pool to join them. "She thinks she spotted a man paying undue attention to her down at the prison, and that he may have taken a picture of her—"

"I don't think." Rosie glanced up at Trent, then pushed to her feet. "I know. He didn't have to stare at me. He was watching me on his phone."

So, still no news about the Bratcher murder. Max played along. Getting her to talk, period, was the first step in getting her to talk about their investigation. "Did you know this guy?"

"I'd recognize him if I saw him again, but I've never seen him before." She backed up onto the patio, keeping both men in sight as Max closed the distance between them. "You don't believe me." She looked across the yard to her neighbors, probably guessing how he'd spent his time back here. Her chin came up as she glanced over at the tall, plastic cabinet, then trained those accusing gray eyes on him. "You never even read the threat, did you? What did Otis and Arlene say to you? You think I'm making this all up."

"I don't know what I think," he answered honestly.

Apparently, that wasn't a good enough answer. With a frustrated huff that might be her interpretation of a curse, she walked past him and opened the cabinet doors. She backed away, picking up the poodle and hugging the dog to her chest, averting her eyes from the shelves inside. "Look for yourself. This is why I called the police."

Max muttered a real expletive when he saw the message and noose hanging inside. He glanced back and scratched around the ears of the little dog who bore an unmistakable resemblance to the toy on display. "Looks a lot like you, killer."

Miss Rosie's eyes widened along with his when his fingertips accidentally brushed against her arm. A split second later she jerked away, pulling herself and the dog beyond his outstretched fingers. "Her name is Trixie. Is someone going to hurt my dogs? Is someone going to hurt me?"

"You don't know who sent this?"

She shook her head and backed another step away.

Right. Not his dog. Not his anything. *Do your job already.* Max busied his hands by snapping a couple of pictures with his phone before pulling out his pocketknife. Trent had come up beside him to inspect the cryptic message. Max asked, "You got a bag in that notebook?"

Trent pulled out a small plastic evidence bag and held it open while Max cut down the threat. The sisal looped around the toy's neck reminded him of the spool of twine Mrs. Dinkle had been using in her garden. He peeked around the cabinet door and caught Arlene watching from her back porch. Otis remained oblivious as she quickly glanced away. Could it be that simple? "Any reason why your neighbors might want to scare you?"

"Because Arlene hates dogs as much as she loves the sound of her own voice?" Max almost grinned at the spunky dig of sarcasm. But Rosie clapped a hand over her mouth. "I'm sorry. That wasn't very polite." She was reining her emotions in again, a skill Max envied, especially today. "The Dinkles aren't responsible for this. And they certainly weren't in Jefferson City snapping pictures of me yesterday. I'm guessing the money from the settlement is the reward that creep is talking about.

Believe me, it doesn't feel like any kind of compensation with all the hassle that has come with it. I'd rather have Mom and Dad and my old teaching job over millions of dollars any day."

I know what you did.

So, who was close enough to Rosemary March, besides her brother locked away in prison, to know or even suspect that she'd murdered Richard Bratcher? Who else cared that she might be guilty?

He plucked the sealed bag from Trent's grasp and dangled it like a pendulum in front of her face. "Can you prove you didn't put this note out here yourself, Rosie?"

Her face went utterly pale. "What?"

"What are you doing, Max?" Trent cautioned.

"Testing a theory." He closed the cabinet doors and moved a step closer. "Have you gotten other threats, Rosie?"

"Yes. Wait. Rosie?" Instead of recoiling from him, she planted her feet, her hand fisting in the dog's curly hair. "We are not friends, Mr. Krolikowski, so you have no right to be so familiar. Or condescending. Especially when it sounds as though you're calling me a liar."

"*Are* you lying, Rosie?"

"Stop calling me that."

"It's a pretty good diversion to make us think someone's after you."

"Diversion from what?" Her chest puffed out, and a blush crept up her neck as understanding dawned. "I'm such an idiot. This is about Richard, isn't it?"

"It's a reasonable question, considering your history. You're kind of like the lady who cries wolf with all your phone calls to 9-1-1."

"My history?" Her cheeks were as rosy as his new nickname for her now. "We're finally getting to the point, aren't we? Is KCPD accusing me of killing him again? Are you accusing Stephen? And here I thought the police had shown up because..." She stared at the evidence bag in his hand for a moment, her chin trembling against the tight clench of her mouth. Then her lips buzzed with an escaping breath and she walked to the gate. "Duchess, heel. Sit." The German shepherd settled onto her haunches beside her mistress, staying put as Rosie opened the gate. Rosie shifted the poodle to one arm and pointed down the driveway with the other. "I'd like you two to leave my home. Now. And please don't gun your engine on your way out of the neighborhood. There's already enough gossip about me without hearing complaints about loud cars leaving my house."

"There's not a damn thing wrong with the way I drive, lady. You and your brother had more motive than anybody to kill Richard Bratcher. I think you'd be less worried about my car and more worried about talking to us and trying to prove your innocence."

She shook her head, probably biting down on some unladylike crack about being innocent until proven guilty. But all he got was a succinct dismissal. "If you won't help me, I'm not helping you. If you gentlemen have any further questions about Richard's murder, you may call my attorney."

Man, that woman was the definition of control. No blowing her stack or shedding a tear or slapping his face. No answers. No freaking reason he should be so perplexed or fascinated by her. He walked up to her, letting his six feet two inches lean in close enough to steal a breath of her summery scent. "Gentlemen? Honey, I'm as far from being—"

"Max, shut up." His partner pushed him on out the gate.

"You, too?" Max patted his chest pocket, but there

was no cigar there. Damn it. The stress, the suspicion, the guilt—too many emotions were hitting him way too fast to deal with them properly. He shook his head and strode toward the Chevelle. "I should have called in sick. I don't need this kind of convoluted drama. Not today." He spun and pointed a finger at the redhead whose cool eyes had locked onto him. "You really need the cops someday, lady, you come and find me. But you'd better be willing to talk and you'd better make sense." He turned and resumed his march toward the car. "I need a drink before I screw anything else up today."

"Excuse us, Miss March. Thank you for your time." Trent hurried to catch up and fall into step beside him. "You know we're not going to get anything out of her now, right?"

"I know."

"You really think she's making up these threats to make her read like a victim instead of a suspect?"

"She's smart enough to do it. Ah, I don't know what I think."

"Hey, Max." A strong hand on his arm stopped him. "I'm on your side, remember?" The tone of Trent's voice was as full of reprimand as it was concern. "It's a little early for the Shamrock, isn't it?"

"Not today, it isn't." He shrugged out of Trent's grip and circled around the car. It was probably best for everybody here—that frightened, pissed-off woman; his best friend; this case; this job; Jimmy's memory; him— if he just walked away.

But something drew his gaze over the roof of the car back to Rosemary March. She'd followed them along the driveway toward the porch, catching the end of their conversation. But she froze as soon as his eyes locked on to hers, one arm hooked around the poodle, the other clinging to the shepherd's collar. From this distance she looked smaller, fragile and as painfully alone as he'd ever been. She'd needed someone to make her feel safe, and he'd chosen to play his bad-cop role to the hilt. He deserved the truckload of regret that dumped on top of the guilt already weighing him down.

Max swung open the car door and climbed inside to start the engine. "Not today."

Chapter Four

Rosemary squeezed her fists around the long straps of her shoulder bag, staring at the steel doors of the elevator while Howard Bratcher rattled on about the trust fund and investment portfolio he and his accountant had put together for her on Stephen's behalf. She'd understood the benefits and restrictions and attorney fees clearly the first time they'd discussed splitting up and managing the settlement money, but it was easier to let him repeat himself than to explain the troubling turn of her thoughts.

Two detectives had come to her home this morning. As if her encounter with that grizzled, grabby, surly Detective Krolikowski and his bigger, quieter partner wasn't upsetting enough, it was dismaying to learn that KCPD had reopened the investigation into her fiancé's murder and considered her and Stephen suspects again. Even six years after she'd found his dead body in his condo, blue faced and frozen midconvulsion, it seemed Richard still had the power to destroy any sense of security and self-worth she'd ever had.

The disturbing phone messages and threat in her own backyard left her as on edge and unsure of the world around her as those last few months with Richard had been. Her morning visit from Detectives Dixon and

Krolikowski had only intensified her feelings of losing control over her own life.

Trent Dixon might have looked like a Mack truck, but he'd been businesslike, pseudofriendly. He'd kept his words polite and had respected her personal space. But Max Krolikowski made no bones about their reason for being there. And despite the military haircut that reminded her so of her father, he'd been coarse, forthright, unapologetically male—not a kindly paternal figure in any way, shape or form.

The broad-shouldered detective with the stubbled jaw and wrinkled shirt was as different from Richard's suit and tie and courtly charm as a man could be. He was right to keep his eyes hidden behind the mask of those sunglasses. On first glimpse, those deep blue irises had been full of ghosts and despair. But upon a closer look, a quick shift in attitude revealed a frightening sort of defiance—as though some great pain was crushing in on him before he summoned his considerable strength or pure cussedness or both and crushed it, instead.

He'd grabbed her, sworn his frustration with a vast vocabulary of objectionable words, accused her of lying, gossiped with the neighbors about her, made friends with her dogs and then invaded her personal space and gone vulgar and insulting again. He couldn't be more unsuited to her guarded sensibilities.

But it wasn't the lack of manners or even the not-so-subtle doubts about her innocence that stuck with her an hour after he'd driven away.

She'd forgotten how warm a man could be.

The heat of the summer sun on his skin mixed with temper and muscle—Max Krolikowski didn't have to touch her for her to be aware of the furnace of heat that man could generate. Yet he *had* touched her, singeing her skin with his abundant warmth. Rosemary wiggled her fingers around the strap of her purse, remembering the shock of his rough hand sliding over her arm. No man who wasn't her brother—she sneaked a glance up at Howard—or a brotherly type, had touched her since long before Richard's death. Frissons of white-hot electricity had danced across her skin beneath the sweep of the detective's hand. She'd reacted to his touch.

And then she'd touched him. Her hand had encountered a wall of warm, immovable muscle when she'd pushed against his chest. For a split second, her fear and fortitude had given way to a reaction that was purely female. Surprisingly aware. Completely out of character for her now.

She remembered closeness. Wanting. She remembered she was a woman.

Rosemary twisted her neck from side to side in discomfort, feeling as if the cold steel walls of this elevator were closing in on her. Why would her hormones suddenly awaken and respond to an ill-mannered beast like Max Krolikowski? Did she have no sense when it came to men? She'd never had a thing for bad boys before. Of course, she hadn't had the chance to have much of a thing for any man. But wasn't rule one that she needed to feel safe? Could it be that six years of isolating herself in order to recapture control over her own life had left her so lonely that any man barging past those meticulously erected barriers was bound to trigger a reaction?

It was all very unsettling. Max Krolikowski was unsettling. Knowing she was still thinking about him, wary of him, curious about him, wondering why Trixie and Duchess had taken to him so readily, was messing with her carefully structured, predictable world.

"We're here." The elevator dipped as it came to a

stop, startling her from her thoughts as much as Howard's interruption had. But by the time the doors slid open, Rosemary had her chin and armor back in place. She arched her back away from the brush of Howard's hand there, hugged her purse to her side and hurried on out the door.

Rosemary stepped out into the cold, modern decor of the Raynard Building's top floor into the Bratcher, Austin & Cole, Attorneys-at-Law, reception area. Before she reached the granite-topped reception counter, Howard wrapped his fingers around her elbow and pulled her to a stop so he could whisper against her ear. "I thought, perhaps, you'd let me take you to lunch afterward."

She didn't immediately process that he'd asked her out on another date, because her mind was too busy comparing the light, cool clasp of his fingers to the purposeful heat of Max Krolikowski's grasp.

Really? She groaned inwardly. Although she couldn't say if her dismay stemmed from her unwanted obsession with the bullying detective or Howard's puppylike determination to turn their relationship into something more than a friendship. How many ways could she say no without hurting his feelings?

Pulling away, she offered him a wry smile. "I don't think that will work today. I've got so much to do at home. There's still a ton of Mom and Dad's stuff to go through."

Howard's smile dimmed. "I understand. Rain check?"

An office door clicked shut at the north end of the hallway and a woman's shrill voice bounced off the sterile walls. "What's she doing here?"

Rosemary's day went from bad to rotten as she turned to face Charleen Grimes. It was impossible not to feel like a frump in the face of the blonde woman's artful makeup and thoroughbred legs. It was impossible not to feel the resentment licking through her veins, either. "Howard is my attorney. Why are *you* here?"

"You don't have to engage her, Rosemary." Howard put his arm around her shoulders and pulled her to his side. This time, she didn't pull away. Nothing like a run-in with her dead fiancé's mistress to sap her strength. "Charleen, what are you doing here?" he demanded with courtroom-like authority. "I thought I made it clear you needed to find different representation."

"You mean besides your brother? I did. I just had an appointment with Mr. Austin." Charleen sauntered across the gray carpet, bringing a cloud of expensive perfume and vitriol Rosemary's way. "You're the one who's got a lot of nerve, showing your face here. I loved Richard. Why couldn't you just let him go?"

After his first attack, Rosemary had been in shock. But after the second time, when he'd twisted her arm so violently it snapped, she'd been more than willing to push Richard Bratcher out of her life. "I told Richard it was over between us. The two of you could have been together. With my blessing."

"Liar."

Rosemary's shoulders pushed against Howard's arm as indignation kicked in. How many people were going to accuse her of that today?

"He pitied you. He said you needed him too much to ever leave you."

What he hadn't wanted to leave was her money. He'd made it clear that he would continue to have Charleen or whomever he pleased in his bed after their marriage because no uptight, inexperienced, overworked mouse like her would ever be able to satisfy a man's appetite. And if Richard's words weren't cruel enough, the slap across the face had been. She'd pulled off his ring and held it out to him. But he'd twisted her arm and the nightmare started.

Rosemary gritted her teeth, blanking the memory of running for her life yet not being able to escape her own home or Richard's torture until he'd run out of cigarettes and had gone for more. "I don't know what to say, Ms. Grimes. Clearly, you're still grieving."

"Grieving? I'm mad because he's dead, and it's your fault."

Apparently, Richard hadn't treated his mistresses like the punching bag she'd been. Rosemary's love for him had died long ago. Why hadn't Charleen's? "It's been six years."

"Feels like yesterday to me. Maybe because two detectives—Watson and Parker—came to my boutique this morning and asked me questions about Richard's death. That's why I'm here—to alert my attorney." Charleen towered over Rosemary with her three-inch heels and movie-star figure. She used that height to her advantage to sneer down her nose at Rosemary. "But I told them who I suspected."

"That's enough, Charleen." Howard removed his arm to clasp Rosemary's shoulders with both hands and turn her to face him. "Is that true? Has KCPD started a new investigation?"

Rosemary shrugged out of his grip. "Why are you asking me?"

The tall blonde laughed. "Because he thinks you did it, too."

"Suzy." Howard snapped his fingers at the receptionist gaping behind her desk. "Escort Ms. Grimes back into Mr. Austin's office."

"But Mr. Austin has a client with—"

"Get her out of here!"

"Yes, sir." The dark-haired receptionist hurried around the stainless counter. "Ms. Grimes, may I take you to the lounge and get you some tea or coffee?"

Rosemary had flinched at Howard's raised voice, but Charleen seemed amused by his anger. "Your brother would never speak to me like that."

"My little brother did a lot of things I didn't approve of." Howard moved his tall body in front of Rosemary, blocking her view of the other woman. "If you want to continue to be a client of this firm, I suggest you learn how to keep your mouth shut and behave like a lady."

"Like boring little Miss March?"

"Do you understand what slander charges are, Charleen? I won't have you accusing Rosemary of something she didn't do."

Rosemary heard a snort of derision. "How do you know she didn't kill Richard?"

Howard's shoulders lifted with a deep breath as Charleen followed the receptionist down the long hallway to the other attorney's office suite. With a hand at Rosemary's back, he escorted her in the opposite direction. Once he closed the door to his inner office behind him, he tried to take Rosemary into his arms. "I'm so sorry the two of you had to run into each other."

But comfort was the last thing she wanted, especially with her temper brewing in her veins. She pushed away from his hug and circled around his desk to look out at the Kansas City skyline. Maybe the world was more normal outside that window. "Six years. I thought…" She crossed her arms in front of her as a shiver ran down her spine. "It was foolish to hope the nightmare of your brother was all behind me. I guess people won't leave me alone until his murder is solved and the real killer is in prison."

Howard shrugged off his suit jacket and draped it over the back of his chair, coming up behind her. "Did the police question you about Richard?"

Rosemary nodded. "Two detectives came to see me this morning, too."

"You should have called me right away. I don't want you talking to the police without me present."

When his hands settled on her shoulders again, Rosemary moved away. "Why? I didn't kill him. I don't have anything to hide." Although she hadn't really answered any of Detective Krolikowski or Dixon's questions once she realized they weren't responding to her complaint about the harassing calls and ugly threat. She stopped her furious pacing and inhaled a calming breath. It was wrong to take her frustration out on her friend. "I'm sorry, Howard. This must all be difficult for you, too. Not knowing who's responsible. I'm guessing the police will be questioning you again, as well."

He waved off her apology and followed her around the desk, where he pushed aside some knickknacks and perched on the corner. "Let them come. My alibi's as solid now as it was six years ago. I'm not worried."

"Still, the memories of your brother—I know you loved him. Our reasons may be different, but you need closure as much as I do."

"I'm so sorry, Rosemary. So sorry for everything. I knew Richard had a temper, but I never knew he was hurting you. Maybe if I had known, I could have done something to stop him. But he was so ambitious, so greedy. He never wanted to put in the time and the hard work to pay his dues and get ahead. He always looked for the shortcut. I guess I thought he'd grow out of it one day. I thought you were a good influence on him, that your marriage would be a success." He glanced toward the door, indicating the confrontation with Charleen Grimes. "You were certainly a better class of woman than those floozies he was always taking to bed. As talented a litigator as he was, he was an embarrassment to the reputation of the firm. Cost us clients. Our father went to his grave thinking Richard was never going to amount to anything worth making him a full partner."

"I don't blame you for anything Richard did. You weren't your brother's keeper."

"Maybe I should have been." He reached for her hand, and she forced herself not to dodge his grasp this time. "I intend to take care of you, though, to make up in some small way for the grief he caused you."

Rosemary managed to drum up a smile of thanks before pulling away. "How about you show me those papers you worked so hard to prepare."

Fifteen minutes later, the papers were signed and she was ready to leave. "I'll drive you home," Howard offered.

But Rosemary slung her purse over her shoulder and urged him back to his chair. "I can call a taxi. I know you have work to do." Besides, she'd already spent most of the patience and socializing she had in her today and needed some time alone to decide how best to manage— or avoid—all this attention suddenly being thrust upon her. She needed to set her emotional armor back into place. "But thank you. And thanks for running interference with Charleen."

He raised her hand to his lips and kissed it. "My pleasure. If you say you didn't kill Richard, then I believe you. And I'll defend your innocence until my dying breath." He tugged her closer and Rosemary put a hand on his stomach to keep him from completing the embrace. Still, he lowered his head to rest his forehead against hers. "Even if you did kill that bastard brother of mine in self-defense or because he deserved it, I'll defend your innocence."

Um, thank you? Her chest tightened at his declaration of support that sounded vaguely as if it wasn't real support at all. Before he could dip his lips to hers, Rosemary pushed away. "I didn't kill Richard."

"Of course not." Why didn't that throwaway remark sound as convincing as it might have even an hour earlier? When Howard circled back to his chair, Rosemary hurried to the door. "I'll talk to you soon."

Not too soon, she hoped. But she kept the thought to herself and closed the office door behind her.

AFTER A WALK with the dogs to maintain their training and give them exercise, several laps in the pool to work her vexation with Howard out of her system, and chicken from her back patio grill for dinner to fill her stomach, Rosemary settled down in the library with a glass of wine to attack another box of family papers and photographs.

Sorting through items from her and Stephen's past, as well as those things that had belonged to her parents, served several purposes. From the most practical—the long-term project gave her something meaningful to do with her time since the suspicion of murder had made it practically impossible to find a teaching job at any certified school. The settlement gave her plenty to live on, but she was a grown woman with two college degrees and a fertile brain. If she couldn't occupy her thoughts and work toward goals, she'd go mad. One of those goals was to possibly sell this place, or at least clear out enough space so she could significantly remodel the interior. There were a lot of good memories here. But there were a lot of bad ones, too. And while the familiarity of her childhood home made it a little easier to cope with the grief, panic and uncertainty of these past few years, there were days like this one when the same-old, same-old felt more like a prison where she was destined to live out her days as the neighborhood pariah—the woman who'd benefited from her parents' deaths, the woman who'd gotten away with murder.

Instead of letting the loneliness and fear take hold, Rosemary plunged into the never-ending—sometimes sentimental, sometimes sad—task of sorting papers, mementoes and heirlooms into piles of things to treasure, items to store or sell and things to throw away.

And so, with the drawn shades and night outside her windows closing her into solitude, Rosemary sat on the thick braided rug in the middle of the library floor, with piles of letters and photographs spread out around her. Duchess stretched out on the cool wood at the edge of the rug while Trixie claimed the couch.

Humming along with the Aaron Copland ballet music playing softly in the background, Rosemary smiled at an image of her father in his Army pilot's uniform, taken a few years before her birth. He'd had that freckled, youthful look for as long as she'd known him, even when his hair had started to gray. Not that the silver strands were that noticeable with his hair cropped so closely to his head. He used to joke that it was time for a trip to the barber if a strand of hair so much as tickled his ear.

Memories of her father drifted to another man with the same broad shoulders and buzz cut. Max Krolikowski was taller than her dad, thick chested and muscular instead of lean and lanky, more tawny haired than strawberry blond. And he certainly lacked that boyish smile. But she could picture the gruff detective dressed in a similar uniform. She could picture him in a gritty, action-packed war movie. What was she thinking? There was nothing fake about Max Krolikowski. She could picture him marching across an asphalt tarmac, boarding a troop transport like the one her father had flown, heading off to fight in a real war.

Rosemary's blood rushed a warning signal to her brain. She shouldn't be picturing the surly detective at all.

With a guilty start, she tucked the tiny snapshot back into the envelope with the letter to her mother. Max Krolikowski was nothing like the quiet gentleman Colonel Stephen March had been. Why couldn't she let her fascination with that rude excuse for a cop go?

Focusing on happier times, she retied the ribbon around the bundle of letters her mother had kept from the correspondence she and her father had traded when he'd been away on his first post after graduating college on his ROTC scholarship. Remembering the love her parents had shared chased away her troublesome thoughts, and Rosemary rose up on her knees to reverently place the love letters in a box marked *Keep*.

She hiked up the wrinkled hem of her dress to crawl over to the box she was sorting and pull out another stack of bound envelopes. But as she sank back onto the rug, her smile faded. "What are these doing here?"

In the chaos surrounding Richard's ultimatums and his subsequent murder, she must have tossed these letters into the wrong box. They weren't correspondence between her mother and father, but a bundle of envelopes from Richard addressed to her.

With her neckline unbuttoned in deference to the

summer humidity, despite the house's air-conditioning, Rosemary mindlessly rubbed her knuckles over her collarbone and the neat dots of puckered scar tissue there. Once, she'd thought it romantic that Richard had sent her notes and poems and pictures, just as her father had sent them to her mother. But now she was wondering why she'd ever kept the tangible reminders of her own foolishness. He hadn't even written the first letter until she'd mentioned how her parents had made such an effort to stay connected when they'd been apart. Now she could see it had all been part of his master plan to make her fall in love and accept his proposal. Weighed down by responsibility and sadness, desperate for someone caring and positive in her life, she must have been an easy mark for a smooth operator like Richard.

"Idiot," she grumbled, reaching out to toss the entire stack into the trash can beside the desk. But then she realized that half of the envelopes hadn't even been opened. A check of the postmarks indicated he'd sent these in the weeks between her breaking off their engagement and filing a restraining order against him, courtesy of his older brother, and Richard's death.

Against her better judgment, she opened the first envelope and pulled out the familiar parchment with the letterhead from his father's law firm. Rosemary shook her head as she read his dramatic scrawl. "I'll end the affair with Charleen. I'll work on my weakness with other women. I love you. I still want to marry you."

There was no apology for the arm he'd put into a cast or the cigarette burns that marred her skin. Not even an acknowledgment of the cruel coercion he'd used to force her to sign the prenup guaranteeing him a share of her settlement money. Just a blithe pronouncement of love. Funny, if she'd been thinking clearly back then, she'd have seen that all the sentences were "I" statements. Maybe if she'd picked up on those egocentric clues when they were first dating, she could have spared herself the mistake of giving her heart to the wrong man.

Rosemary returned the letter to its envelope and reached for her wineglass to wash away the taste of disgust with a crisp pinot grigio. The trash was too good for these reminders of that sick relationship, so she dropped it and the rest of his letters into a box and set it aside. This winter, she'd burn them with the first fire in the fireplace. She smiled as she raised the goblet to her lips to take a sip.

But a flicker of shadow in the window behind her reflected off the glass.

Her stomach clenched. Wine sloshed over her hand as she spun around. Nothing. Just the blinds swaying with the current of air blowing from the AC vent. She inhaled a deep breath, willing her heart rate to slow down.

Probably just the headlights of a car driving past.

But then Duchess lifted her head, growling a low warning in her throat. Trixie jumped to her feet and barked, startling Rosemary. "What is it?"

She set down the wineglass with a trembling hand, running a quick mental check. Doors locked. Windows locked. Alarm system armed. Lights on. Dogs at her—

Rosemary screamed at the explosion of shattering glass outside. Trixie sprang from the couch as Duchess leaped to her feet. Both dogs dashed to the front door. A man-size shadow darted past the blinds. Someone was on her front porch. Why didn't the alarm go off?

The dogs' frantic barking nearly drowned out the second explosion of smashing glass. The translucent light filtering through the blinds suddenly went dark and she realized someone out there was breaking the lights. Pounding on the porch railing and furniture outside.

Avoiding the door. Avoiding the windows. Avoiding doing any damage that would trigger a siren and flashing lights.

Shrinking away from the assault on her house, Rosie screamed again at the crunch of metal on metal. "Stop it." She hugged her arms around her waist. "Stop it!"

But a crystal-clear moment of clarity fired through her brain, snapping her out of her chilled stupor. What if the intruder smashed through the door next and turned whatever weapon he was using on her dogs?

Or on her?

A wailing alarm couldn't help her then.

Rosemary lowered her hands into fists. "Duchess! Trixie!"

The barking paused for a second, then started up again, warning away the intruder at their door. Rosemary snatched her cell phone off the desk and ran into the hallway, grabbing their leashes off a foyer chair and joining the canine alarm. "I'm calling the police!" she shouted. "Get out of here! Now!"

Footsteps pounded across the slats of her porch and faded into silence. The man was running away. "Duchess, sit. Come here, Trix."

As silence fell outside, Rosemary regained control of the dogs. Kneeling between them, she hooked them up to their leashes and pulled them back from the door. Did she dare unlock it to see what was going on? Trixie, especially, was ready to charge whatever danger was on the other side of that door, and Duchess's low-pitched growl indicated that no one here felt entirely safe. She almost wished it was a random act of vandalism or attempted burglary. But she'd dealt with too many threats these past few days to believe she was anything but the intended target. She transferred both leashes to her left hand and pulled out her cell, her thumb hovering above the 9 on her screen.

But was calling KCPD again really an option for her? Was there any cop out there willing to help a murder suspect?

Rosemary pocketed her phone and waited a good two minutes, until the growling subsided and she got Trixie to sit beside the bigger dog. That meant whoever had been on her porch was long gone. It was safe to open the door, right?

Ignoring the thumping pound of her heart inside her chest, Rosemary typed in the disarm code, unhooked the chain and dead bolt and twisted the doorknob. Still in her bare feet, she stayed inside the locked storm door to survey the damage. There was shattered glass everywhere. A broken table. The intruder had taken a bat or crowbar or some other heavy object to the lights on either side of her door, plunging her porch into darkness. But there was enough light shining out from the foyer to see the dented black metal mailbox hanging by a screw from the siding beside the door.

Once she was certain the intruder had left, she pulled the leashes taut and nudged open the storm door.

"Oh, my God."

There was enough light to read the note hanging from the flap of her mailbox, too.

Murdering whore.
Justice will be done.

She swayed on her feet, shock making her light-headed for a moment. Her landline rang in the house behind her and she jerked in surprise, sending the dogs into another barking frenzy.

Avoiding the broken glass beneath bare feet and dog paws, she pulled Duchess and Trixie back into the house and locked the storm door. After the fourth ring, the machine in the kitchen picked up, and a man's garbled voice echoed like a creepy whisper throughout the house. "I can see you, Rosemary. I know you're alone. Those dogs can't protect you. I know you're afraid."

The shiver that shook her body nearly robbed her of breath. She didn't remember slamming the front door or releasing the dogs or pulling her cell from the pocket of her dress.

But some shred of a memory stopped her from completing the 9-1-1 call.

KCPD had blown off her last report of a threat. She didn't need anyone patronizing her fears—she needed to feel safe. She wanted to prove to the police she wasn't lying—that she was the victim now, just as she'd been six years ago. With the dogs at her heels, Rosemary ran to the answering machine at the back of the house. But she had no intention of picking up the phone or even erasing that sick message. She had no intention of dealing with Dispatch and being put on hold or winding up as a footnote on some report.

Instead, she pulled the phone book from beneath the machine and looked up an address.

She knew where she could find at least one cop tonight.

Chapter Five

Max swallowed a drink of beer that had lost its chill and set the mug down on the rim of the pool table at the Shamrock Bar. He leaned over, blinking his bleary eyes and lining up the shot, tuning out the drone of conversations around the room and the jingle of the bell over the bar's front door. "Six in the corner pocket."

He tapped the cue ball and grinned as the pink ball caromed off the rail and rolled into its target. Finally, something was going right today.

He'd circled to the end of the table to assess his best angle for dropping the seven ball before realizing the noise level of the thinning crowd had paused in a momentary hush. Even his opponent on the opposite side of the pool table seemed to have frozen for a split second in time.

"She's new." Hudson Kramer, a young cop with a shiny new promotion and the subsequent pay hike burning a hole in his pocket, lay down his cue stick and combed his fingers through his hair as glasses clinked and conversations started up again. Was the game over? Hud's mouth widened with a lopsided grin as his eyes tracked movement behind Max. "Wonder if she's lost. Maybe she needs a friend to help her find her way."

With Kramer's grumble of protest at having his shot

at winning back the money he'd lost tonight interrupted, Max turned and saw the last person he'd ever expect to see in a bar. "I'll be damned."

Rosemary March's copper-red hair was pulled back in a bun that wasn't anywhere as neat and tidy and screaming *old maid* as it had been this morning. *Fire and ice.* The unexpected metaphor buzzed through his head at the sight of several loose, wavy red strands bouncing against her pale cheeks and neck as she moved. The idea of her letting all that hair flow freely around her shoulders and tunneling his fingers into a handful of it hit him like a sucker punch to the gut. Max sat back on the edge of the table, propping his cue stick against the floor to hold himself upright as she approached.

He must have had too much to drink and was conjuring up hallucinations. He closed his eyes and muttered a curse, wondering why he wasn't conjuring up images of babes on swimsuit calendars instead of Miss Priss with the sharp tongue and crazy ideas.

He opened his eyes again. Nope. She was real. And she was excusing her way past a couple of tables and a cocktail waitress, heading straight toward him and the pool tables. She'd exchanged the dressy sandals for a pair of flip-flops, but she still wore that white, high-necked dress from this morning, looking as virginal and out of place in a bar at this hour as he'd felt at her house this morning. Didn't mean she didn't look all kinds of pretty to a half drunk, half horny bastard like him.

"Ah, hell," he muttered again, wishing he'd said no to that last beer so he could control that little rush of misplaced excitement at realizing she'd come to see him.

"Detective Krolikowski?" She stopped a couple of feet in front of him, her fingers tightening around the strap of the purse she hugged in front of her. Mistaking his dumbfounded silence for a lack of recognition, she tilted those dove-gray eyes to his and introduced herself. "Rosemary March? We met this morning? I'm not armed, I promise."

"I know who you are, Rosie. You here for a drink?" When the waitress slid between the redhead and the nearest table, Max automatically reached out. Rosie pried at his hand when he tugged on the strap of her purse to pull her out of the other woman's path. Her hips jostled between the vee of his legs and his thigh muscles bunched in a helpless response to her unintentionally intimate touch there. Max instantly popped his grip open and let her scoot around his leg into the space beside him. Ignoring his body's traitorous response to a warm, curvy woman, he held up two fingers to capture the waitress's attention. "Wait. You probably want something fancier than a beer. Wine? One of those girly things with an umbrella?"

"Nothing, thank you."

Oh, he was in a bad way today. After waving off the drink order, he turned on the edge of the pool table and pulled a long, copper-red wave away from the dewy perspiration on Rosie's neck. Warm from her skin, he rubbed the silky strand between his thumb and fingers. "So is this you lettin' your hair down? You go to a bar, but you don't drink? Or is this a temperance lecture for me? Couldn't get enough of puttin' me in my place this morning, eh?"

"No, I… What are you doing?" She jerked away, snatching her hair from his fingertips and tucking it behind her ear. "This was a dumb idea."

Max pushed to his feet and thumped the tip of his cue stick on the table in front of her, blocking her escape. "Hold on, Rosie Posy. What *are* you doing here?"

Her shoulders lifted with a deep breath and she turned, staring at the collar of his shirt before tilting her wary eyes up to his. "I overheard you and your partner talk about coming here. The Shamrock Bar. I looked up the address in the phone book."

"Do you ever give a straight answer to a question?" He hunched down to look her right in the eye. "That's how you found me. Now tell me what you want. Let me guess—you're a pool hustler, and you're here to win ten bucks off me to spite me for being such a jerk this morning."

Hud Kramer walked up behind her before the shocked O of her mouth could spit out an answer. "I bet she could take you, Max."

Max bristled at the interruption. Why was that kid grinning? "Shut up."

Rosie turned to include both men in her answer. Sort of. If looking from one chin to the other counted. What was that woman's aversion to making direct eye contact? With that tart tongue of hers, he couldn't really call her shy. But something had to be going on to make her subvert that red-haired temper and any other emotion she might be feeling. "I haven't played for a long time. I used to be pretty decent back in college when I'd go out with friends, but I don't think I'd win."

"I'd be happy to give you a few tips, Red." The younger cop seemed to take any answer as encouragement to his lame flirtations. "Aren't you going to introduce us, Max?"

But when Hud leaned in, Rosie flinched back, maybe sidling closer to what was familiar, if not necessarily what she considered friendly. Max shifted in an instinctively protective response, and her hair tangled with the scruff of beard on his chin, releasing her warm summer scent. His pulse leaped and he was inhaling a deep breath before he could stop himself. Rosie March might be a baffling mix of mystery and frustration, but she exuded a wholesome, flowery fragrance that was far more intoxicating than the beer he'd been drinking.

Max growled, irritated by how much he noticed about this woman. And he was even more irritated that the younger detective had noticed it, too. "Get out of here, Kramer."

A soft nudge to the chest with Max's pool cue backed Hud up a step, but the young hotshot was still smiling. Yes, the woman had rebuffed him in favor of the older detective who needed a shave and an attitude adjustment. But Hud wasn't about to lose to him twice in one night. "Our game isn't finished, Krolikowski. I have a feeling I'm about to make a comeback."

Groaning at the taunt, Max set his cue stick on the table and pulled out his wallet. He reached around Rosie to hand a ten-dollar bill to the young officer. "Here. Take it."

"You're conceding defeat?"

"I'm conceding that you annoy the hell out of me and I'm tired of puttin' up with you. Now scram."

"Yes, sir." Kramer took the sawbuck with a wink and a mock salute and headed straight to a green vinyl seat in front of the polished walnut bar to order a refill.

With more room to avoid him now, Rosie quickly stepped away and moved around the corner of the table. "I'm sorry you lost your money. That wasn't my intention." She pulled open the flap on her purse and pulled out her wallet. "I only wanted to talk to a police officer."

Now she wanted to answer questions? Max scanned the booths and tables around the bar. "Take your pick.

The majority of the men and women here work in some kind of law enforcement."

"Could I talk to *you*?"

He looked down to see her holding out a ten-dollar bill. Muttering a curse, he pushed the money back into her purse. At this late hour, every young stud in the place was looking for any unattached females who might be interested in one last drink and a chance to get lucky. They wouldn't know that Rosie was a person of interest in a murder investigation. They wouldn't care about her eccentricities or that she could rub a man wrong in every possible way. Like Kramer, they were noticing the outward appearance of innocence and vulnerability. They were seeing the promise of passion in the red flag of Rosemary March's hair. Maybe they were picturing what it would look like down and loose about her bare shoulders, too.

Even in his hazy brain, Max knew she didn't belong here.

"Let's get out of here. Robbie?" He looked to the Shamrock's bearded owner at the bar, and tossed some bills on the table to pay for his tab. "Come on."

Grabbing Rosie by the arm, he turned her toward the door. Whatever she wanted from him, he wasn't about to go toe-to-toe with some young buck who wanted to pick her up just for the privilege of finding out. Although she hurried her steps beside him to keep up, she tried to shuck off his grip. But Max tightened his fingers around her surprisingly firm upper arm muscles and didn't let go until he'd ushered her out the front door into the muggy haze of the hot summer night.

He took her past the green neon sign in the front window so that curious eyes inside wouldn't get the idea that she might be coming back before he released her. He plucked a fresh cigar from his shirt pocket and leaned back against the warm bricks. "Now talk to me."

Once he released her, she took a couple more steps and turned. "You smoke?"

"Not exactly." He tore off the wrapper and stuffed the plastic into his pocket. Then he held the stogie up to his nose, breathing in the rich tobacco scent until he could rid the distracting memory of fresh summer sunshine from his senses. Light from the street lamps and green neon sign in the window reflected off the oily asphalt of the street behind her, making her seem even more out of place in the dingy surroundings. At least he didn't have to deal with Kramer or anybody else hittin' on her out here. Max set the cigar between his teeth and chomped down on it. "Make sense, and make it fast, okay?"

He watched the reprimand on her lips start and die. Good. He wasn't in the mood for one of her lectures on the evils of swearing and smoking—one of which he hadn't done for years. She seemed to consider his request for brevity and nodded. "Actually, I want you to come to my house. I had a trespasser tonight. I don't know how long he was there before he started vandalizing my front porch. He broke the lights and left a message in my mailbox. It's…disturbing, to say the least." She reached into her purse and pulled out a folded sheet of white paper with just her thumb and forefinger and held it out to him. "It's typed like the one I found on the back patio. No signature to say who it's from."

Straightening from the wall, Max snatched the paper from her fingers and unfolded it. "Somebody threaten your dogs again?"

Her chin shot up and her cheeks dotted with color. "He's not after my dogs. He just knows they're a way to get to me. To scare me."

"You keep saying *he.*"

"Or she. I don't know who it was. All I saw was the shadow on my porch and the damage after the dogs' barking scared him away."

Max squinted the words on the note into focus. "Murdering whore. Justice will be done." Anger surged through his veins and he swore around the cigar. "You should have reported this ASAP to 9-1-1 instead of taking the time to track me down."

"I don't want to be brushed off with another phone call, and I certainly don't want to be accused of making it up again."

"What makes you think I'm gonna believe you?"

Her tongue darted out to moisten her lips, and his pulse leaped with a response that told him he was already far too interested in this woman to remain objective. Probably why he was such a growly butt around her. He didn't want to like her. It didn't make sense to like her. And yet, she was doing all kinds of crazy things to his brain and libido.

"To look at you, and listen to the way you talk… You're military, aren't you? Or you used to be? Not just the haircut. But, the way you stand. The way you move. You recognized Dad's gun as Army issue, and you remind me of him when he was young. Except, he was shorter. More patient. And he didn't smoke."

Hell. Where was she going with this? Suspicion tried to move past the fog of alcohol and put him on alert.

"Dad was in the Army. A career man who retired as a colonel. Isn't there some band of brothers code I can call on for you to help me? Without treating me like a suspect in a murder case?"

Max tilted his face to the canopy of cloudy haze reflecting the city lights overhead. He'd spent the day mourning his fallen band of brothers, cursing his inability to save them all—to save his best friend. He couldn't do this. He couldn't call on that part of him to do his duty and fail again. Not for this woman. Not for a comrade in arms or superior officer he'd never even met. With a self-preserving resolve, he lowered his gaze to hers and handed back the note. "You should have called Trent. He's the reasonable one."

"No one will listen to reason." Her hands fisted in frustration. "I need someone who'll help me out of blind faith in my innocence…or out of a sense of duty. Or honor. Besides, I don't know where your partner is. But I remembered you said you were coming here for a drink."

"That was this morning. What made you think I'd still be here?" A little frown dimple appeared between her eyebrows when she wrinkled up her nose in an unspoken apology. Oh. Her opinion of him was that low, huh? He supposed he'd earned it. And yet she'd sought him out instead of Trent or one of the other off-duty detectives and uniforms inside the cop bar. Maybe he shouldn't alter her opinion of him by telling her he'd gone back to his desk at the precinct and put in his full shift before grabbing a burger and heading to the Shamrock. "How will me going to your place prove you didn't put this note there, too?"

The soft gaze that had held his for so long dropped to his chin. Her skin blanched to a shade of alabaster that absorbed the harsh green color of the neon sign. He didn't like that unnatural color on her. He didn't like feeling like a first-class rat for blanking the color from her skin.

"Hey, I…" Max pulled his cigar from his mouth with one hand and reached for a red tendril with the other. Although she startled at his touch, she didn't immediately pull away this time. Instead, she watched his hand as he sifted the silky copper through his fingers. "I'm sorry, Rosie. I'm having a really sucky day. It's hard to see the good in anything or anybody tonight."

"You're not always like this?"

He chuckled at the doubtful face she made. "Some say I am. But on this one day every year, I'm an extra sorry SOB."

"I wish you wouldn't swear like that. I get that you're angry, already."

Oh, he was angry, all right. At himself. At friends who died. At failing to save them.

"I get that you're hurting. Did something bad happen?"

"Yeah. Something very bad happened. To a friend of mine." She'd tilted her eyes up to his, bravely held his gaze. Maybe it was a trick of the lights and shadows, but from this angle, standing this close, her eyes filled with compassion, maybe even a little of that same odd awareness he'd been feeling about her. A man could lose himself in the deep, soft shadows of her eyes if he wasn't careful. As uncomfortable with her intuition about him as he was with the male interest stirring deep inside him, he pulled his fingers from her hair and retreated. "You said your daddy served?"

She nodded, retreating a step herself. "He flew troop transports and cargo planes until he retired from active duty. Later, he commanded a local unit in the National Guard."

Max thought of the unseen pilots and navigators who'd flown him, Jimmy and the rest of their battered squad from the Middle East into Germany. Another transport had finally brought them and the caskets of their fallen friends stateside. The world was a mighty small place in some ways. "He flew soldiers home?"

"Sometimes. Is that important?"

Those pretty, intuitive eyes snuck right past his survival armor. An image of Jimmy's frozen dark eyes blipped through his thoughts. *Never leave a man behind.* He crushed the memory that left him reeling and grabbed her arm, pulling her into step beside him and striding down the sidewalk. "Where's your car? I'll walk you to it and then follow you back to your house."

But when he stepped off the curb he stumbled. His momentum pulled her against his chest for a split second, imprinting his body from neck to thigh with her warm curves, filling his head with that damnable clean scent he wanted to bury himself in.

"On second thought, maybe you'd better drive."

She was the one who grabbed a fistful of shirt and his shoulder to steady him and guide him back to the sidewalk. "You're drunk, aren't you?"

There was that snappy, righteous tone again. Her eyes had gone cold. "That was my goal, honey. It helps me forget."

Rosie didn't waste any time pushing away. "This was a mistake. I thought you were different."

"You are the most confounding woman…" With his emotions off the chart, his hormones twisted up in a mix of lustful curiosity and a craving for the peaceful solace he'd read in her eyes—not to mention the four beers he'd drunk since dinner—Max tossed his unlit cigar into the gutter and stopped her from walking away. "Did something scare you tonight or not?"

He spun her around and pulled her up onto her toes, bringing her lips close enough to steal a kiss if he wanted to. And, by hell, he wanted to.

Shifting his hands to the copper bounty of her hair, Max tunneled his fingers into the silky waves and pulled her mouth to his. With a gasp of surprise, her lips parted and Max took advantage of the sudden softening of that preachy mouth by capturing her lower lip between his. He drew his tongue along the supple curve, tasting something tart and lemony there. Her lip trembled at his hungry exploration. He felt the tiny tremor like a timid caress and throttled back on his blind need. Another breath whispered across his cheek, and he waited for the shove against his chest. But her fingers tightened in the front of his shirt, instead, pressing little fingerprints into the muscles of his chest, and she pushed her lips softly against his mouth, returning the kiss.

Something twisted and hard, full of rage and regret, unknotted inside him at her unexpected acceptance of his desire. Frustration faded. Anger disappeared. The wounds of guilt and grief that had been festering inside him all day calmed beneath her tender response. He threaded his fingers into the loose twist of her bun, pushing aside pins and easing the taut style until her hair was sifting between his fingers and his palms were cupping the gentle curve of her head. "Your hair's too pretty to keep it tied up the way you do, Rosie. Too sexy."

"Detective Krol—" He kissed her temple, her forehead, reclaimed her lips once more. He'd reached for her in a haze of frustration and desire, but she was holding on with a gentle grasp and angling her mouth beneath his. It wasn't a passionate kiss. It wasn't seductive or stylized. It was an honest kiss. It was the kind of kiss a man was lucky to get once or twice in his life. It was a perfect kiss. Beauty was taming the beast.

Or merely distracting him?

Detective?

Ah, hell. He quickly released her and backed away, his hands raised in apology. "Did something scare you tonight…besides me?"

"You didn't scare me," she lied. Her fingers hovered in the air for a few seconds before she clasped them around the strap of her purse.

Max scraped his palm over the top of his head, willing his thoughts to clear. "Just answer the damn question."

She nodded.

She wasn't here for the man. She was here for the cop. He'd like to blame the booze that had lowered his inhibitions and done away with his common sense, but fuzzy headed or sober, he knew he'd crossed too many lines with Rosie March today. "I think this is where you slap my face and call me some rotten name."

Her eyes opened wide. "I wouldn't do that."

"No, I don't suppose a lady like you would."

Her lips were pink and slightly swollen from his beard stubble. Her hair was a sexy muss, and part of him wanted nothing more than to kiss her again, to bury his nose in her scent and see if she would wind her arms around his neck and align her body to his as neatly as their mouths had fit together. But she was hugging her arms around her waist instead of him, pressing that pretty mouth back into its tightly controlled line. When had he ever hauled off and kissed a woman like that? With her history, she'd probably been frightened by his behavior and had given him what she thought he wanted in hopes of appeasing him, counting the seconds until he let her slip away. She had to be terrified, desperate, to come to him after this morning's encounter. The fact that she wasn't running away from him right now had to be a testament to her strength—or just how desperate she was to have someone from KCPD believe in her. And, for some reason, she'd chosen him to be her hero.

Max scrubbed his palm over his jaw. He hadn't played hero for anybody in a long time. He hadn't been any good at it since Jimmy's suicide. He did his job, period. He didn't care. He didn't get involved. This woman was waking impulses in him that were so rusty from lack of use that it caused him pain to feel himself wanting to respond to her request. "What do you need from me?"

She tucked that glorious fall of hair behind her ears and tried to smooth it back into submission. "I think I'm in real trouble. And I don't know what to do. KCPD thinks I might be a killer, so they're not taking me seriously and won't look into these threats. But I thought that you…maybe you'd set aside your suspicions and do it for my dad. I know it's an imposition, and I know you'd rather be investigating me for murder than deal with some unknown stalker you think I made up, but—"

"You're right, Rosie. I was a soldier. Sergeant First Class, US Army. A man like your dad brought me and my buddies home from a hell of a fight where we lost too many good men." For the first time in a lot of months, on that flight across the Atlantic, he'd been able to close his eyes and sleep eight hours straight, knowing he and his men were safe from the enemy as long as they were on that plane. "What was your daddy's name?"

"Colonel Stephen March."

"Maybe I don't owe the colonel personally. But I owe." She'd appealed to the soldier in him, tapped into that sense of duty he'd once answered without hesitation. She had him pegged a lot sooner than he was figuring her out. "And I owe you for putting up with me on my worst day."

"Is there something I can do to help? Besides…" She

ran her tongue around her lips, maybe still tasting some of the need he'd stamped there. "I'm a very good listener."

He grumbled a wry laugh. So, no offer to repeat that kiss, eh? "Just give me a chance to be a better man than the one you met today."

"You'll come look? You'll help me?"

Either he was the world's biggest sucker, or Rosie March was in real danger and she believed he was her best chance at staying safe. Whether he was doing this for her or her dad or to atone for all the mistakes he'd made today—all the mistakes he'd made in the past eight years—he was doing it. "Yes, ma'am." Wisely keeping his hands to himself this time, he gestured for her to lead the way to her car. "Let's go find this lowlife."

Chapter Six

"Why do you swear so much?" Rosemary glanced away from the stoplight to the big, looming silence sitting beside her in the passenger seat of her car. Although the beard stubble on his square jaw took on a burnished glow from the lights from the dashboard, Max Krolikowski's craggy face remained hidden in shadows. And while she normally appreciated the absence of any confrontation, ten miles without one word left her questioning the wisdom of this last-resort plan to seek him out as an ally.

"Like you said. I'm angry."

And hurting. He said something bad had happened to a friend. If there was one thing she understood about people, it was the stages of pain and grief a person went through when he or she lost someone or something very dear to them. She'd gone through them with her parents, her brother's drug use and murder conviction. Her relationship with Richard. Denial. Anger. Sadness. Acceptance. Only, Max Krolikowski seemed to be stuck in an endless loop of anger and pain.

The light changed and she drove through the intersection. His fingers drummed a silent rhythm on the armrest of the car door. Was that endless tapping an indication that his temper was still simmering beneath the surface? She remembered those strong fingers tangled in her hair, holding her mouth beneath his. He'd used words like *pretty* and *sexy*—and she'd believed him. For that moment, at least.

Richard had never used words like that with her. She'd looked nice. She'd do him proud at a family dinner or business luncheon. And Richard's embraces had never been so spontaneous, so unabashedly sensual.

When Max Krolikowski kissed her, she'd felt that knee-jerk instinct to flee from the unfamiliar, from the potential danger of the unknown. But she'd felt something else, too. She'd felt need. She'd felt heartache. She'd sensed a hopeless man discovering some shred of hope.

Or maybe she was the one who'd succumbed to the need to be held and wanted and important to someone— even for a few seconds outside a noisy bar. Because once he'd gentled his kiss, once she understood there was something besides anger driving his embrace, she'd become a willing participant. A shyly eager partner. Out of her depth, perhaps, but not afraid.

There was something bold, raw and honest about Max's emotions that was completely foreign in her experience with men. But she'd take that kind of blunt honesty, that disruptive force of nature, over Richard's cool charm any day. Richard's cruelty had been a blindside waiting to happen. At least with Detective Krolikowski, she knew to expect the unexpected.

Which brought her thoughts around to the question she'd really wanted to ask. "Why did you kiss me?"

"I saw the chance. I took it. It seemed like the right thing to do at the time."

And now? Did he still think she was…kissable? Rosemary's hands tightened around the steering wheel as the next question came out in a throaty whisper. "Is that what you want from me?"

The drumming stopped. "You mean like payment for helping you out?" He muttered a succinct curse.

"Language, Detective."

"Wow. Your opinion of me must be lower than I thought." His voice was deep and resonant and laced with contempt. "Don't lecture me on my mouth and insult me at the same time. If you're going to treat me like a degenerate, I might as well talk like one."

Rosemary's grip pulsed around the wheel as a defensive temper flared in her veins. "I wasn't insulting you. I'm just trying to understand what's happening between us. My experience with men is rather limited, and hasn't been entirely positive. I haven't had control over a lot that's happened in my life. And now some creep is trying to undermine what little sense of security I do have." She glanced across the seat and found deep blue eyes bearing down on her. She quickly turned her attention back to the neighborhood streets and took a deep breath to cool her outburst and resume an even tone. "I need to understand so I won't be caught off guard again. As for the swearing? If you need to use those words to get your emotions out, then go ahead, I'll get used to it. But they remind me of someone I'd rather not think of."

"Bratcher? Is that how he talked to you?"

The accuracy of his guess made the scars on her chest burn with remembered terror of her erudite fiancé transforming into Mr. Hyde. She rubbed at her collarbone through the linen dress she wore, willing the memories to subside before they could take hold. Max waited with surprising patience until she nodded. "Ninety percent of the time, Richard was the perfect gentleman. But sometimes, in private, he'd blow up."

"Probably when you had a difference of opinion or you tried to assert yourself?"

Rosemary exhaled a breath that buzzed her lips, her temper cooling to match the facade. Max was sounding more like a cop now. And with the finger of suspicion pointed elsewhere for a change, she found his questions easier to answer. "Once he put that ring on my finger, he changed. I knew then it was just about the money. He didn't love me. I didn't realize just how much he loved that settlement money, though."

"Rosie, I'm not aiming any of those words at you, and I don't mean to offend you. It's just I'm a bull in a china shop and you're a piece of china."

She had the scars, inside and out, to scoff at half of that idea. "I'm not fragile. It's just…I'd rather not hear them."

His disbelieving laugh was a deep, hearty tone from his barrel chest. "Yes, ma'am. I'll try to do better."

Despite the suspicion that he might be mocking her, Rosemary nodded her thanks. "That's all I ask."

They drove an entire block before he surprised her by continuing the conversation. "I wasn't thinking when I kissed you, either. I was just doing what felt right at that moment. Look, I admit, I've had a few drinks, and I'm not that great at filtering my thoughts and emotions in the first place. You smelled good."

She *smelled* good? How could such a simple phrase feel as flattering as being called *pretty* or *sexy*? Frankly, she thought she might need a shower after the stress and heat of the day. But his words made her lips tighten against the urge to grin.

He shrugged, his big shoulders seeming to fill the empty space inside her car as he searched for more of an explanation. She could feel the warmth emanating from his body when he turned in his seat to face her and gripped the wheel more tightly to keep from leaning toward it.

"Rosie, I didn't analyze it. I felt like kissing you. The opportunity was there, so I did."

After this morning's battle of wills, she'd been certain the rather earthy Max Krolikowski wouldn't give her a second look—unless he was throwing darts at her picture. "I didn't think I was your type."

"Neither did I." He sank back into his seat with a low exhale. His eyes drifted shut. "Don't worry. I won't let it happen again. I'm a cop, doing the job I should have done this morning. I'm not expecting any favors from you."

Now, why did that reassurance kill any urge to smile? Ignoring her uncalled-for disappointment, Rosemary turned her car into the driveway and shut off the engine. When she saw the dark expanse of her porch and heard the dogs barking inside, it was easy to remember that she'd asked him here to help with the threats, not the loneliness. "We're here. I didn't touch anything except for the note." She pointed to the street lamp behind them. "There's a little light from the street, but if you need a flashlight, there's one in the glove compartment."

He pulled out the flashlight and tested it before shutting the compartment and climbing out. When he hesitated outside his door, Rosemary did the same. He scrubbed his hand across his jaw, a habit that drew her attention to its firm, square shape and the intriguing mix of tawny, gold and brown stubble there. Richard had always been clean-shaven. But Max's day-old beard had been a sharp contrast against her softer skin. His beard had been ticklish, abrading, stimulating—his lips and tongue had been soothing in the aftermath.

Fortunately, he spoke before she succumbed to the silly urge to run her tongue across her lips, remembering what he'd felt like there.

"You know, if you get mad at me, I'm not going to hurt you like Bratcher did. I know I talk loud and need to clean up my act, but I would never lay a hand on you in anger." His gaze found hers when she didn't immediately respond. "I'm not going to leave, either. I said I'd help, and I promise to do what I can."

"For my dad."

He opened his mouth to say something, but changed his mind and circled around the hood of her car, ending the conversation and slipping into detective mode. "Yeah. For your dad. Hooah."

HUA. Heard. Understood. Acknowledged.

Nodding at the military acknowledgment she remembered her dad using, Rosemary followed him up onto the porch. When Max stumbled over the top step, she instinctively reached out to help him. But he caught her arm instead, urging her back behind him while he swept the beam of light over the upended rocking chair, splintered wood and shattered glass littering her porch. "Son of a—" He bit off the curse and released her. "Somebody was smart enough to avoid triggering the alarm—or else plain lucky. This is a lot of rage. Who blames you for your fiancé's death?"

"Who doesn't?" He swung the light over to her, hiding his opinion of her flippant remark in the shadows. Rosemary shook her head, not understanding how a dead man could still be wreaking so much havoc in her world. "I wasn't holding Richard to any promises. I broke off our engagement. I wanted him out of my life."

"Murder is a permanent way to do that."

She pushed the flashlight aside to look him in the

eye. "How many times do I have to say it? I did not kill Richard. The only reason I was at his condo that morning was to tell him to stop threatening Stephen with trumped-up charges. He thought blackmailing me would convince me to take him back, but Howard, my new attorney, helped me get a restraining order. I wanted to deliver it to him myself—prove that he couldn't intimidate me anymore."

"But you didn't get to say any of that. You found him dead?"

She nodded, squeezing her eyes shut against the horrible memory of Richard's dead, discolored body. But his puffy blue lips weren't the only detail she recalled. She hugged her arms around her waist before opening her eyes and looking up at Max again. "I could tell he'd been there with another woman. There were condoms on the nightstand and her perfume was still in the bedding."

"He cheated on you, threatened you, abused you. A jury would see that as a lot of motive to kill a man." At her wounded sigh, Max's big hand clamped around hers before she could storm away. "But I'll start working on the assumption that you didn't. Maybe we can track down this other woman. See what she knows."

She remembered her confrontation with Charleen Grimes that morning. Charleen had been so certain that Rosemary was responsible for ending her lover's life. Could that have been a show to hide her own culpability? There'd certainly been plenty of witnesses to her accusations. Still, why would Charleen want to kill the man she professed to love? Rosemary had a feeling the affair had been a tempestuous one. But poison wasn't exactly a spur-of-the moment weapon.

"Rosie?" Max's growly voice interrupted her thoughts. "If you know who the other woman was, I'm going to need that information. The best way to prove your innocence is to find out who really killed your ex."

Rosemary tugged her hand from his grasp and tried to gauge the sincerity of his words. "You believe me?"

"I promised to help."

Not exactly a rousing vote of confidence. But she was scared enough to take it. She gestured to the mess on her porch. "Do you at least believe I'm not doing this to myself?"

"I think I need a clearer head to make sense of what's going on here." He swung the flashlight toward the sound of the dogs barking behind the door. "Sounds like they need to get out and run around. You got coffee?"

"I can make a pot."

"Do it. Give the dogs a few minutes outside, then keep them in the house with you. Wait. We'll go in through the back. I want to get pictures of the damage before anything is moved. I want to bag that note of yours, too."

He made no attempt to touch her again but fell into step beside her to walk her down the driveway. With every passing second, he was becoming more cop, more man of duty, rather than the tipsy desperado who'd pulled her into his arms and kissed her because he thought it was a good idea at the time. She should be grateful for his professionalism, for the distance he put between them now. That would make it easier to keep her guard up and stay focused on the problems she needed to deal with.

"You got a toolbox somewhere?" he asked, waiting for her to unlock the back door.

"Yes. Dad's workbench is still out in the garage."

"Then I'll need it open, too." After she gave him the pass code, he waited for her to air the dogs, even tussling a little bit with Duchess and Trixie himself, before urging them all back into the house and telling her to lock the door.

Rosemary fed the dogs a treat, brewed a fresh pot of coffee and pulled the makings for a simple sandwich from her fridge.

An hour later, she carried the last of the coffee to the front door to refill Max's mug before she washed the dishes. She could do this. She could grab his plate and fill his mug and get back to the kitchen without getting herself into any uncomfortable conversation or unwanted physical contact with the man. Although the dogs were eager to spend more time with their new friend on the porch, she shooed them behind her before stepping out to find Max putting the finishing touches on replacing her mailbox.

"Want the last cup?" she offered.

"Sure. I'm going to have a whale of a headache in the morning, but the food and caffeine help." He nodded toward the empty mug and plate on the bench he'd moved beside the rocking chair to replace the broken table.

"Is that a thank-you?" she asked, wondering if there were any manners lurking under that tough hide of his.

"Yeah." He paused with his hand in her father's toolbox, then faced her. She'd like to think that was a blush of humility on his cheeks, but she suspected the flush of color in the shadows was due to the hard work and the temperature that had barely cooled at one in the morning. "You didn't have to go to the extra trouble, but I appreciate it."

"You're welcome." Relaxing enough to smile at the unexpected compliment, she nodded toward the twin glare of bare lightbulbs on either side of her front door. "You didn't have to go to all this trouble, either. I'm grateful. But that wasn't why I asked you here."

"I've always liked working with my hands. Keeps me out of trouble," he added without any elaboration, before plucking a screw from his pocket and going back to the job at hand. "You'll have to get new globes to cover the bulbs I replaced, but everything is cleaned up and secure. As soon as I finish this."

"Uh-huh." Rosemary didn't move. So much for keeping a polite distance and hurrying back into the house. Max's shirt had come untucked somewhere along the course of the long day. And as he raised his arms to drill in the last screw, his shirttails lifted up and his jeans slipped a tad, giving her a glimpse of his gun and badge and a set of abs that belied the beer he claimed to have consumed tonight. She knew he was brawny. She expected him to be fit working for the police department. But the holstered weapon and strong male body beneath the wrinkled clothes and antisocial attitude made her a little nervous.

Although she couldn't say if the suddenly wary tempo of her heart stemmed from the clear reminder that Max was a cop, and cops ultimately treated her as a suspect rather than a victim—no matter how nice they were being about fixing the vandalism on her front porch. Or maybe those tingles of awareness of a man were a real attraction, fed by the unanswered questions she still had about that kiss. When she realized her gaze was lingering on the thin strip of elastic waistband peeking above his belt, she snapped her gaping mouth shut and turned her attention to refilling his mug.

A relationship was the last thing she wanted, right? Richard had made it perfectly clear that she was too timid, too plain, too boring, to ever turn a man's head to thoughts of passion. She was far better suited to domesticity and duty than she was to warming a man's bed or heart. And though, logically, she knew his cruel words had been used to break her spirit and manipulate her, the sting of self-doubt reared its ugly head whenever she noticed a man as something other than a friend or acquaintance. Why set herself up for disappointment and humiliation when the most attractive quality she had, according to Richard, was the money in her bank account?

A relationship with Max Krolikowski could be especially problematic since he seemed to be even less refined, led more by his instincts and whatever he was feeling at any given moment than Richard had ever been, pushing her even more out of her comfort zone and making him a real enigma in her limited experience with the opposite sex.

Not that Max was offering any kind of a relationship. He wasn't interested in her money. He wasn't particularly interested in being here at all. Max was here because he'd been in the Army like her dad. He was a creature of duty as much as she was. A soldier would do for another soldier or his family.

And a military family would do for a soldier in need.

Rosemary put down the plate she'd retrieved, and set the coffeepot beside it. Far better to clear the air between them than to muddy the waters with some foolish fantasy that wasn't going to happen. Clinging to the rocking chair he'd righted, she faced him again. "What happened to your friend? Is it something that interferes with your work a lot?"

Max removed the bit and carefully laid the drill back in her father's toolbox and closed the lid. For a moment she didn't think he was going to answer. Then he crossed into the shadows near the porch railing and sat, crossing his arms in front of him, looking big and unassailable. "You're determined to talk about this, hmm?"

Rosemary withdrew behind the chair. "I believe, maybe, if we're going to be working together, we need to."

"You think this is going to be a team effort?"

"I know you have more questions for me. I don't expect you to help me for nothing—"

"Relax, Rosie." He dipped his face into the light, his sober blue eyes drilling straight into hers. "I'll help you—you help me. Just go easy on the lectures and the heart-to-hearts and remember—I'm giving you fair warning. You can't fix me."

"Are you broken?"

His eyes narrowed and his head jerked slightly, as if her question surprised him…or struck a nerve. Muttering one choice word, he sat back against the porch post. "You're not the only one who's lost people you care about. Eight years ago today, I lost my best friend. Captain James Stecher. We served together in the Middle East."

"He died in battle?"

"Nope. Stateside. Shot himself. Post-traumatic stress."

"Oh, Max." His blunt answer made her eyes gritty with tears. She reached out to squeeze his hand or hug away the pain she imagined hiding behind that matter-of-fact tone.

"I thought it was *detective*."

The growl of sarcasm and his stalwart posture made him seem impervious to pain—or at least unaffected by her compassion—so she curled her fingers around the back of the rocking chair instead. "I'm sorry."

"For what? I'm the one who screwed up. I should have been able to save him."

He rose and leaned across the chair to pick up his coffee. Rosemary managed not to jump when his body heat brushed past her. But when he straightened beside her—tall, broad, the sleeve of his cotton shirt brushing against her shoulder and raising goose bumps—she couldn't help retreating a step.

"I've decided I'm not going to make the same mistake with you," he said.

"What does that mean?"

"It means I need you to drive me to my car at the Shamrock. Then I'll follow you back here and sit out front the rest of the night." He turned and doffed a salute to the shadow in the Dinkles' window she hadn't noticed until that moment. She gasped as the shadow disappeared, and the blinds swayed with Otis or Arlene's hasty retreat. "You've already got the neighbors' attention by bringing me here. I'm guessing you don't entertain a lot of men."

She lifted her panicked gaze to his. She hadn't even noticed the Dinkles' curiosity, but Max had probably been aware of her nosy neighbor the entire time. "Do you think that's necessary? I just wanted a police officer to see what was happening to me and write a report."

"I intend to do more than that, Rosie."

Her blood ran cold at the ominous portent in his voice. "Do you think something else is going to happen?"

"I'm not going to give whoever this bastard is a chance to scare you again. Or do something worse. There's only so much guilt a man can live with." He continued to scan the neighborhood from her dark porch, even though the Dinkles' spying had been temporarily thwarted. He picked up the note he'd sealed in one of her plastic sandwich bags. "If Bratcher's killer is behind these threats, he or she could be doing it to divert suspicion onto you. Keeping an eye on you might ferret out the suspect."

"I see." Rosemary understood the logic, even if she didn't relish the idea of playing the part of bait for KCPD. Shivering now, she hugged her arms around her middle. "So watching over me and what happens here helps your investigation?"

"Possibly." He reached out and rubbed his hand up and down her bare arm, eliciting more goose bumps as her skin warmed beneath even that casual touch. "But that's not the only reason. If this guy is someone who blames you for Bratcher's murder and thinks they're meting out some kind of justice…?" He lifted his fingers to her hair, scowling at the lone tendril falling against her neck as if he didn't like that she'd pinned the rest of it up into a practical bun again. His palm settled along her jaw, and, instinctively, against her better judgment, she leaned into his warmth. "Look, the only thing you have to understand about me is this. I'm not losing anyone else on my watch. You're still my team's best shot at solving this case. If something happens to you, chances are, we'll never uncover the truth."

If something happens? Even the heat from his callous hand wasn't enough to erase the chill crawling over her body. So volunteering to watch over her wasn't personal at all. It was a practical move on his part. She should appreciate practicality. But the no-nonsense offer hurt, made her wish she hadn't gone to him for help, after all.

Pulling away, Rosemary crossed to the front railing and looked to the street, picturing Max's car parked beside the curb. A man with a gun and a baby blue muscle car should draw all kinds of attention to her quiet home. Attention she didn't want. "What exactly are you saying? You're going to stake out my house every night until you finish your investigation? You're just going to wait until this guy makes good on one of his threats?"

She felt his breath against her neck as he walked up behind her. Her eyes drifted shut at the unintentional caress. But it wasn't reassurance he was offering. "Actually, I was thinking more along the lines of moving into your basement apartment. Your neighbors, this stalker, and possibly the killer, are already going to question why I'm here. But they might drop their guard a little bit if they think I'm the new tenant."

Rosemary scooted away from the warmth she craved. "But that's Stephen's apartment."

"He's not going to be using it for a few years." He caught her by the wrist and turned her to face him, his stony expression telling her his idea wasn't really up for debate. "We're talking a matter of weeks, maybe even days, that I'd be here. I get that I overstepped some personal boundaries and made you uncomfortable earlier, but my plan makes sense. I'll clear it with my team leader tomorrow."

"What if I say no?"

"Why would you say no?" He leaned in, close enough for the moonlight to pick up the color of his eyes and make them glow like a predatory cat as he glared down at her. "I thought you wanted to uncover the truth as much as KCPD does."

"I do." She tugged her wrist free and folded her hands together, willing him to understand the inviolate need to maintain the one place of sanctuary she had left in the world. "But I'm not comfortable having a man in the house. Even with the separate entrance, it would feel like I'm locked in there with you and I wouldn't be free to come and go when I want to. You're laying down rules. You're taking over my life."

"You came to me for help. Do you want to catch a killer or not?" He pointed to the trash bag with the mess from the vandalism he'd cleaned up. "Do you want this sh—" He caught himself, held up a hand in impatient apology and changed the word. "Do you want this garbage to stop? I don't care how many locks you have on that door, if this guy escalates any further, you won't have time to wait for help to get here."

She dropped her gaze to the middle button on that broad chest and considered how helpless she would be against Max's strength if he ever decided to turn on her the way Richard had. She'd thought she could hide in the sanctuary of her own room, lock Richard out. But even without Max's muscular build and physical training, Richard had been able to kick down her door, destroy her phone before she could call for help and hold her hostage for several hours. Repeated threats against her brother had been enough to keep her from pressing charges later. She absently rubbed her palm over the scars on her chest, drifting back to that horrible night.

But two blunt-tipped fingers sneaked beneath Rosemary's chin and tipped her face up, forcing her back to the moment. Max's stern face hovered above hers. "Rosie, I'm not any good at guessing games or reading between the lines. You look me in the eye and tell me exactly what you want."

A dozen different wishes popped into her head. She wanted the memories of Richard's abuse erased from her mind and body. She wanted Max Krolikowski to kiss her again. No, she wanted the sober detective gently touching her skin to *want* to kiss her. She wanted the self-assurance that Richard had stolen from her so she could tell Max all the wishes running through her mind. She wanted her parents alive and her brother safely home from prison. Ultimately, though, there was only one thing that mattered.

"I want to feel safe."

With a firm nod, Max dismissed any further discussion. He picked up the toolbox and the trash bag and paused in front of her. "Then this guy won't get to you again. I'll need a key. I'll need you to do what I say, when I say it. And I'll need you to trust me."

"I know you mean that to be reassuring, but…" She trudged back into the house and locked the door when he indicated that he was heading around to the garage and she shouldn't remain outside by herself. She whispered against the door as she threw the dead bolt. "That's what Richard said, too."

Chapter Seven

Max recognized Olivia Watson's short, dark hair as she waited to get on the elevator at KCPD headquarters to report for their morning shift. Thank goodness. He hated running late.

Despite the throbbing in his temples left over from last night's trip to the Shamrock Bar, Max jogged across the foyer's marble tiles. "Hey, Liv. Hold the elevator."

"Good morning, Max." The brunette detective smiled a friendly greeting as he slipped in beside her and headed to the back railing. He leaned his hips against it, exhaling a deep breath. She pointed to the wraparound sunglasses he was still wearing. "The lights too bright in here for you?" she teased.

Great. Trent must have blabbed about him drowning his sorrows last night. And Liv here, like a mother hen to her boys on the Cold Case Squad, couldn't resist making sure he was all right. Max was a grown man, the oldest member of the team. He didn't need any mama or sister or busybody sticking her nose into his regrets. Time to play the old boyfriend/former-partner-who'd-nearly-ruined-her-career card. "Detective Cutie-Pie giving you any grief? Or do you still need me to punch him out for you?"

But Olivia refused the bait and punched the button for

the third floor. "I think I finally got it through Detective Brower's thick skull that I don't love him, nor does he even remotely turn my head anymore." She raised her left hand and wiggled her fingers in front of his face. "Of course, the engagement ring Gabe gave me makes a clear statement as to where my heart and loyalties lie."

Max grabbed her wrist to get a better look at the respectable rock on the plain gold band on her third finger. "Hey, congratulations, kiddo." He let her go and leaned in to kiss her cheek. "So that pesky reporter is finally going to make an honest woman out of you."

"Gabe is not pesky."

Max shrugged. "I suppose he did help us catch a killer and put Leland Asher in prison. But reporters who bad-mouth the department still aren't my favorite people."

She leaned against the back wall beside him and jabbed him with her elbow. "Hey. Gabe has printed some nice things about KCPD now, too. He's honest. Always tells it like it is—whether it's good press or not. It's why I trust him. It's one of the things I love best about him."

He nudged her back. "As long as he makes you happy."

"He does."

If Max had any family besides his grandma, he'd wish it included an annoying "sister" like Olivia. Of course, she already had three big brothers, a father and grandfather looking out for her. If Gabe Knight passed muster with her family and she was genuinely happy with this guy, then so was Max. "Then I guess I'll put up with him."

"Do you own a suit and tie?"

He let his head fall back and groaned. "Why?"

"Because I'm inviting you to the wedding."

"You ask a lot of a man, don't you?"

"Only the ones I care about and respect." She reached over and tapped his cheek. "I like the clean-shaven look this morning. Remember how to do that for the wedding. What's the occasion?"

He was glad the elevator had stopped and the door was opening. He'd shaved for work more than once this week. Or maybe that was last week. Had he spruced up in an effort to redeem himself in the eyes of a certain critical redhead? "Hell."

Olivia followed him out into the morning bustle of the third-floor detectives' division as the shifts changed from third watch to first watch. "So what makes you grouchy with an extra side of cranky this morning?"

Trent Dixon was there to meet them as they checked in at the sergeant's desk. "One too many beers last night, I'll bet." Before Max guessed the younger man's intent, Trent had snatched the sunglasses off his face. "Yep. I swung by your apartment this morning to make sure you got here. But nobody answered."

Max snatched the glasses back and hooked them behind his neck. "Did you break in to see my bed hadn't been slept in?" he groused.

"That's for amateurs." He patted the shield on his belt. "I've got one of these, remember? All I had to do was ask nicely. Your super let me in." Trent and Olivia both grinned as they led the way past their desks to the break room for a morning cup of joe.

But Max knew his partner's concern was real. "I left early. Had an errand to run. I dozed a couple hours in my car."

"In your car?" When Max stopped in the hallway outside the break room, Trent and Olivia did, too. Trent was serious when he came back and clapped a hand on Max's shoulder. "But today's a new day?"

Max nodded. His annual Jimmy funk was out of his system—or at least relegated to the backseat in the carful of sticky issues he had to deal with. He looked from one detective to the other, letting them know this wasn't the hangover talking. "I think I got us a lead on the Richard Bratcher murder case. Not from the source you might expect. I was following up on it. Remember our little interview gone south yesterday?"

Trent snickered. "Rosemary March? Is she suing us? Filing harassment charges against you?"

Max rubbed his knuckles over the unfamiliar smoothness of his jaw. She probably would if he tried to kiss her again. Not that he had any plans to do so. In the sane, sober light of day, he…was wondering if any part of Rosie's gentle response had been real. Man, he was going to have to keep his wits about him and his hormones in check on this mission. "I'm going to be spending a lot of time with her over the next few days."

"Come again?" Trent asked.

They were all in cop mode now, listening.

"Turns out her dad was military, and she's latched on to that aspect of me. She looked me up last night to help with a problem." He glibly skipped past the whole kissing, sparks flying, guilt trip gone sideways incident outside the Shamrock and filled them in on the vile message and rage-fueled destruction he'd tried to repair for her. "Rosie's stalker is legit. And he's escalating. She could turn out to be a good witness for us, but not if this guy gets to her first."

"Rosie?" Liv asked, looking to Trent for an explanation. "You mean Stephen March's sister?" Olivia had no love for Rosie's brother since his efforts to cover up the murder he'd committed had involved several attempts on Olivia and her new fiancé's life. "When did she become Rosie?"

With a shrug, Trent gestured to Max, indicating he had no clue why his partner would give a cutesy nickname to the person who'd been not only the prime suspect, but the only suspect, period, in the initial investigation of Richard Bratcher's murder six years ago.

"It's just what I call her, okay?" Max wasn't about to explain anything personal to either of them, especially since he couldn't pinpoint why *Rosemary* didn't seem to fit the woman who'd gotten so far under his skin yesterday. *Rosemary* was a murder suspect. A mission objective to be explored and dealt with.

Rosie was, well, he wasn't quite sure. And while part of him wanted to blame last night's kiss and desire to get involved with her problems on an unfortunate mix of beer, lust, loneliness and guilt, Max was afraid his connection to Rosie went a little deeper than a cop doing his duty. That whole band-of-brothers logic she'd used to justify seeking him out had only sealed the deal.

Whether he had his team's backing or not, he'd given his word that he would help Rosie unmask her stalker. But finding the bastard who terrorized a vulnerable woman would be a hell of a lot easier if he had the Cold Case Squad and resources of KCPD backing him up.

Ignoring the question, Max stuck with talking copspeak to Trent and Olivia. *That* he understood. "The timing of these threats is suspect. Either someone connected to the murder is trying to point the finger at her to keep us from looking at them, or someone who knew Bratcher blames her for his death, and is punishing her for it since we haven't arrested anyone for the crime yet. I documented the evidence last night at her house. Rosie couldn't have done that kind of damage herself unless she was doped up on something. With her brother's history of drug abuse and an aversion to drinking, smoking and swearing, I'm guessing she doesn't get high."

"Wait a minute," Trent interrupted, nudging Max and Liv to a private corner as the hallway filled with A-shift cops reporting to the conference room for Morning Roll Call. "You went back to her house?"

"Would you believe she picked me up at the Shamrock Bar?" Trent's expression indicated not. "Close your mouth, junior." Here was the really incredulous part. "Apparently, Rosie thinks I can be her hero. Watching her house, doing what I can to catch this guy who's terrorizing her, should get me close enough to get the answers we need from her. I think she knows more names linked to Bratcher we haven't found yet. I believe she can give us leads that'll make this cold case hot again. If she can't break open this investigation for us, then I have a feeling the guy who's after her will." Max braced his hands at his waist, looking up to Trent and down at Liv to include them both. "I don't think I can do this on my own, though. I have to sleep sometime. Plus, I'll need a liaison to Katie—" the team's information specialist "—and all her records when I'm out in the field. And somebody has to be with Rosie 24/7 while I'm following up some of those leads."

"Whatever you need, brother," Trent offered. "If Miss March turns out to be the linchpin to this investigation, I'm sure Lieutenant Rafferty-Taylor will want the whole team involved."

Olivia agreed. "I'll go brief Jim." Jim Parker was her partner, another member of KCPD's Cold Case Squad. "Are you sure we can trust her, Max?"

"I didn't think so at first, but yeah. I think she's being straight with me." Max's measurements of the dents in the mailbox and light sconces made him think the perp's weapon of choice had been a metal baseball bat. If he'd chosen to take a swing at Rosie or one of the dogs defending her, KCPD would have been investigating something far more serious than vandalism. "I'm hoping my word is enough for you guys to let me run with this."

Liv nodded. "You guys covered for Gabe and me when we needed backup. So you know I'm there for you." When she reached up to brush an unseen greeblie off the shoulder of his shirt, Max wondered if he'd really needed neatening up, or if—with all the other detectives and uniforms filing into the room across the hall—that was her professional version of a supportive hug. "See you two at the morning meeting."

Max grabbed a cup of coffee and followed Trent into the conference room. Weaving through men and women gathered in conversations between the long, narrow tables facing the captain's podium, they found two open chairs near the back of the room.

Max had barely raised the paper cup to his lips when Trent slapped his leather folder on the table and leaned over to ask, "You sure you can do this? Yesterday, Rosemary March was a whack job, and today the *old prune* you couldn't wait to get away from is *Rosie*, and you're going to be her knight in shining armor. Why the change of heart?"

Max raised his gaze to the curious officer eavesdropping on their conversation from the opposite side of the table. The young man with the nosy intent turned out to be Hudson Kramer from the Shamrock Bar. "Did you score with that redhead last night, Krolikowski?"

"Sit down, junior, and mind your own business."

"You struck out, huh?" Grinning like a schoolkid,

Kramer braced his hands on the table and leaned closer. "S'pose I could get her number?"

"No, I don't suppose you could." Raising his hands in mock surrender, the younger detective wisely turned away and took his seat before Max lowered his cup and glanced over at his partner. "You don't think I can handle this mission...er, assignment?"

"Max, you are the toughest SOB I know. You can make anything work if you set your mind to it." Trent rested an elbow on the table and thumped Max in the chest. "But I also know you're a pussycat in there. Your emotions get the better of you sometimes. Hell, if Kramer's razzing can rile you, then I've got to wonder just what Rosemary March means to you."

"She's a solid lead on our case. And somebody's got her in his sights." Max downed another sip of the hot brew. "I'm protecting a potential witness. I'm doing my job."

"Uh-huh. I can deal with the crazy guy once a year on the anniversary of Jimmy's death, and cover for you." The conversations around the room receded into background noise when Trent dropped his voice to a whisper. "But if you don't do some healing, if digging up Rosemary's secrets is going to keep you stressed around the clock and you start flipping out again, the lieutenant is going to order a mandatory psych eval on you. You could get suspended if you wig out on the job again, or you start hitting the Shamrock every night. You're too good a cop for that—too good a man. I don't want to see you lose it."

"That's mostly why I'm doin' it." Yeah, as if stepping up to be that pretty, prickly woman's bodyguard was some kind of therapy for him. More like penance. Still, it felt like the right thing to do. "I didn't save Jimmy."

Max sat up at attention, his posture reflecting his resolve. "But I'm damn straight going to save her. I'm gonna make things right in this world for once."

"And solve Bratcher's murder?"

Captain Hendricks took his place at the podium and the room instantly quieted. The black man swept his gaze across the room, greeting them all. "Good morning."

"Yeah. Sure," Max muttered beneath the other officers' responses. "That's the idea."

An hour later Max was on his second meeting of the day and his third cup of coffee, sitting through a Skype call between drug research expert and CEO Dr. Hillary Wells of Endicott Global, a drug company based in the KC area, and the other members of the Cold Case Squad.

The brunette woman with short hair and a white lab coat over the business suit she wore filled up the viewing screen in Ginny Rafferty-Taylor's office. Lieutenant Rafferty-Taylor was the veteran detective who headed up the Cold Case Squad. Dr. Wells and the lieutenant seemed to be about the same age, and both were successful professional women. That was probably why Dr. Wells's answers were all directed to the lieutenant. Everyone else in the room seemed to be beneath her time and interest.

"RUD-317 is a cancer-fighting drug," the woman on the screen explained. She seemed more interested in fiddling with the jar of hand cream on her desk than in the interview. "It's not for recreational use."

"Our victim wasn't a cancer patient, Doctor," the lieutenant clarified. "And if he used drugs recreationally, he kept it private. We have no arrests or complaints on record."

"His file says he was a smoker," Trent pointed out. "Is

it possible our guy got private treatment? A diagnosis in a foreign country not in his US records? He had money. Maybe the cure worked."

Dr. Wells barely spared a glance for Max's partner. "It's possible. RUD-317 is available in other countries." She glanced down at her notes on her office desk. "I'd have to double-check the status to see if that was true six years ago." She raised her dark eyes to Lieutenant Rafferty-Taylor again. "We've never seen side effects like you describe with RUD-317. I wonder if your victim had an allergic reaction to something in the formula. Or perhaps there was a bad combination of drugs in his system. We do have specific protocols in place for using the RUD products."

The lieutenant might be a petite little blonde, but she was tough as nails, and Max respected her for it. She wasn't going to let the other woman dismiss their case. "Dr. Wells, there are too many other circumstances related to the death of this particular victim for KCPD to readily dismiss it as an accidental drug overdose. We're looking at it as a homicide."

"I see." Dr. Wells jotted something on her notes. "If you fax me a copy of the medical examiner's report, I'd be happy to take a look at it to confirm her conclusions or add to it if any discrepancies jump out at me."

"We'll do that. Thank you, Dr. Wells."

The brunette woman leaned toward the camera, her face filling the screen. "I'd certainly hate for bad publicity surrounding one of Endicott Global's medical products to get out. Trust me, the board of directors is always on me about maintaining Endicott's public image. If one of our company's drugs was used to commit a murder, I want to know about it. Its misuse might require altering our product labeling and warnings so it doesn't happen again accidentally. We might even have to pull the drug off the market. You know how prevalent lawsuits are nowadays. People can make a fortune and ruin a company that does good work."

Max shifted uncomfortably in his seat at the mention of lawsuits. They were nothing but trouble. It didn't look as though Miss Rosie Posy's nine million dollars were doing her any good.

"I'll have one of my detectives get in touch with you to follow up."

The lieutenant ended the call and Max was back to justifying his plan to the other members of the Cold Case Squad. "Rosemary March wouldn't give us anything yesterday," he explained. "She's not that comfortable with cops."

Lieutenant Rafferty-Taylor arched a silvery-blond eyebrow at him. "So what's your *in*?"

He looked to the woman sitting at the head of the conference table and shrugged. "I remind her of her dad."

"Ouch." Jim Parker, Olivia's partner and the newest member of the team, made a face across the table. "You're not that much older than she is. That has to be hard on the ego."

Max skimmed his hand over the top of his jarhead haircut. "Former military."

Jim got serious and nodded his understanding. "She trusted her father, and so she trusts you."

"Something like that." Max set his cup down beside the stack of case files in front of him and pulled out a photograph of Richard Bratcher to set on top. "I believe she's as anxious to solve Bratcher's murder as we are. This guy made her life hell when he was alive. He's been dead six years and he's still doing the same."

Olivia Watson rested her elbows on the table and

leaned forward. "And she thinks finding the killer will make her stalker go away? Could whoever is after her be the real murderer, trying to frame her?"

"That's one idea I had," Max agreed. "Either that, or we've got an unsub who thinks she did it and got away with killing Bratcher."

"So, we need to be interviewing people who were close to Bratcher besides the Marches." Olivia sat back. "Do we have anyone on that list?"

"I'm working the stalker angle." Katie Rinaldi, the brunette information specialist assigned to the team, looked up from her laptop at the far end of the table. "I've been surfing social media sites, trying to track down the pictures Miss March alleges were taken of her when she visited her brother in Jeff City."

"Find anything?" Max asked, suspecting that Rosie was a private enough woman that she wouldn't willingly put herself out on the internet.

Katie's ponytail bobbed behind her as she shook her head. "Nothing yet except for some newspaper photos related to winning that settlement on her parents' behalf, Mr. Bratcher's death and her brother's sentencing for murder." She lifted her blue eyes to include everyone around the table. "But I'm just getting started. I've got some facial recognition software I'll plug in and run against other sites. If her stalker posted pics anywhere, I'll find them and forward the info to your phones and computers."

"Good idea," Jim said, his expression turning grim. "That's how those crooked cops down in Falls City where I worked undercover tracked down my wife. Through a simple picture from our first date she posted online. This guy ain't playin' if he's gotten that close to your witness."

Lieutenant Rafferty-Taylor agreed. "That's a good strategy, Katie. If there are unsanctioned pictures of Miss March online, I want to know who put them there."

"Yes, ma'am."

The lieutenant turned her attention to the big man sitting beside Max. "Trent, let's get those written threats and telephone messages Miss March has received in for analysis. See if any of them are traceable."

"Will do."

Max nodded, appreciating the team following his lead and treating Rosie as a threatened witness instead of a suspect. He tapped the case files on the table in front of him. "I talked her into coming in this morning to look at some photos from known associates of Leland Asher and the vic. Maybe she can ID the guy she saw that way."

Ginny Rafferty-Taylor was a sharp thinker who'd solved several homicide investigations before accepting the promotion to head up the Cold Case Squad. She allowed her team to run with their instincts but demanded their ideas be backed up with hard facts. "We're still working on the theory that several of KCPD's unsolved cases are related?"

They'd had this same discussion several months earlier, when Olivia had closed the six-year-old murder of Danielle Reese, the investigative reporter Stephen March had killed—the crime he was now serving time for in Jefferson City. Although Max's focus was on one woman and one case, he had to agree the idea of connected murders had merit. "It could have happened that way. The Marches had a strong motive for eliminating Richard Bratcher, yet Rosie lacked the means and Stephen lacked the opportunity. We've got Stephen March for murdering Ms. Reese even though Leland Asher and his organization are the ones with the motive for killing her. Asher had an alibi for the night of that murder."

The lieutenant tucked a short, silvery-blond lock behind her ear. "Does Asher have an alibi for the night of Bratcher's murder?"

"I'd love to ask him," Olivia volunteered. "I hate that he's serving a mere two years in prison. Maybe we can make his stay more permanent. If he's behind any of this, we should be able to get a list of contacts he's had recently. Jim and I can look at the prison's visitor logs."

Jim nodded. "We'll find out who he's close to on the inside, too."

Katie Rinaldi tapped her finger against her lips. "It's like that Hitchcock movie, *Strangers on a Train*—you kill the person I want dead and I'll kill yours, and no one will ever be able to prove a thing."

The possibility of the seemingly unrelated murders having a common link had been Olivia's idea to begin with. "There has to be a connection between Leland Asher and the Marches or Bratcher we can find."

Katie ran with the idea. "What if there's a third murder involved that connects everything? Or a fourth or a fifth?"

Trent rolled his chair away from the table and spun toward Katie. "Why don't we stay away from the movies and focus on reality. If we can get Rosemary March on board, I'm sure we can find facts to solve Bratcher's murder and make our case."

Bristling at the criticism, Katie put her hands back on the keyboard and typed a note. "I'll do the research in my spare time—start cross-checking all unsolved murders from the last decade or so. If I find something… *when* I find where those unsolved murders overlap, I'll let you know."

"When do you have spare time?" Trent grumbled. "You're either working or doing something with Tyler and your family or doing one of those stupid plays."

"It's a hobby." Katie's eyes flashed with temper, although her tone remained politely articulate. "And I've made some new friends by getting involved with the community theater. I'm allowed to have a hobby."

Not when it took time away from any possibility of Trent and the single mom spending time together rekindling their high school sweetheart relationship. Max turned away to hide the shaking of his head, happy to leave the soap opera of young love to those who had the energy and fortitude to deal with it. Cupid could just keep his arrows away from a confirmed ol' bachelor like him, and let him do his job and get from one day to the next without any more hassle than necessary.

And yet… Max looked through the window separating Lieutenant Rafferty-Taylor's office from the main floor and saw Rosie March and a tall guy in a fancy suit following one of the uniforms past the maze of detectives' desks toward a row of interview rooms. He was half-aware of other strategies being discussed around the table, of assignments being given. But he was more aware of how the bright flowers printed on Rosie's black dress warmed the pale perfection of her skin. Although the high neckline and modest hem of the sleeveless dress covered up all the interesting bits of her figure, and that old-lady bun at her nape made his fingers itch to free her hair again, there was a distinctive tightening behind his zipper that couldn't be blamed on the desire to drown his sorrows in alcohol or any willing woman this morning.

Stone-cold sober, the dutiful daughter of a colonel was still gettin' to him like an irritation beneath his skin. Could he be just as distracted by the undercurrents of tension between him and Rosie as those that had flared between Trent and Katie a few moments earlier?

Apparently so. Max's hand curled into a fist beneath the table when Rosie startled and drifted back a step, hugging that long shoulder bag to her chest as Hudson Kramer jumped up from his desk to greet her and the suit guy with the silver sideburns. The irritation running beneath Max's collar felt an awful lot like jealousy when he saw Kramer turning on the charm. What did that kid see in Rosie? Was Kramer into that cougar thing? Did he have a penchant for redheads? Or...

Nine million dollars?

The other hand fisted beneath the table. If Hud Kramer had recognized Rosie from the newspaper and thought he could sweet-talk his way into a few dates and a little payout—

"Brother." Trent clamped a hand down on the arm of Max's chair and shook him out of his glowering stare. His partner was kind enough to point toward Lieutenant Rafferty-Taylor, who'd also noticed his straying focus.

With a nod to Max, silently welcoming him back to the meeting, the petite lieutenant continued her summary. "Let's follow up on the toxin that killed Bratcher, too. Sooner rather than later. Endicott Global is big business. If they're worried about bad publicity that might come from being tied to Bratcher's murder, I don't want to give Hillary Wells or anyone else there a chance to scrub their records from six years ago." The lieutenant glanced at the notes on her computer screen. "And if they can give us new information that might not show up on the ME's report, I want to know that, too. With Jim and Liv on the road to Jefferson City, and Trent on forensic evidence detail, Max, I'll leave that to you?"

He jotted the directive in his notebook. "Yes, ma'am."

The lieutenant closed her laptop and stood. "Very well. You've got point on this, Max. Get whatever you can out of Miss March. Use Trent as your contact, and keep us in the loop for any kind of backup or research you need."

Max nodded, then pushed his chair back the moment they were dismissed, eager to get to Rosie to verify that the plan they'd agreed to last night was still in place. He scooped photos and reports and stuffed the files into his binder to sort out later.

He hadn't even made it around the corner of the table when he stopped in his tracks. But it wasn't the young stud wannabe chatting up Rosie that rankled this time. "Who does that guy who came in with Rosie look like to you?"

"An attorney?"

Max picked up the photo of Richard Bratcher and tossed it onto the table in front of Trent. "Look again."

Trent picked up the picture and whistled under his breath. "An older version of our vic. Now that's awkward." He rose to his feet beside Max. "They're looking pretty chummy. You think the two of them could have plotted together to kill Richard?"

Max didn't want to think that Rosie had plotted anything. But a partner in crime turning on her could certainly explain the stalker. A man who wanted revenge on the woman he thought killed his brother would, too. "I think I'd better go introduce myself."

Trent grinned as Max headed out the door. "Call me if she throws something at you or threatens a lawsuit."

Hud Kramer took the stack of mug shot books the uniformed officer had been carrying, and led Rosie and the other man to the closest interview room. Max dumped his binder on his desk, ignoring the papers that spilled out, and quickened his stride to catch up to the group when Rosie hesitated in the doorway and the ringer for their dead guy nudged her on inside.

"She's not going to like that little room," Max muttered, catching the door before it closed in his face. He pushed it open and stepped inside, looking first to those pretty gray eyes that zeroed in on him and widened before her gaze shuttered and she looked down at the table that cut the room in half. Hell. He'd agreed to help her, hadn't he? Why was she still shying away from him? More important, why did it bother him so much that she did? Max turned his attention to Kramer. "I've got this."

"I was just doing the heavy lifting." Seriously? The younger detective made a point of flexing his muscles when he set down the thick books. "I was keeping the lady occupied until you got out of your meeting."

Max pointed a thumb over his shoulder. "Get out of here and go do some real police work."

"Yes, sir. Bye, ma'am." He winked at Rosie on his way out, earning a soft smile.

"Thank you, Detective Kramer," she answered. Max's groan of annoyance faded when Rosie lifted her gaze to him again. Better. He liked it when he could see into the cool depths of those pretty eyes. But that look was far from a come-on, and her succinct tone reminded him of the reason she was here. "Good morning, Max."

"Morning. You want to introduce me to your friend?"

"Of course." She gestured to the man beside her. "Detective Krolikowski—this is my attorney, Howard Bratcher."

Max extended his hand but hesitated midintroduction. This guy was definitely going on the suspect list. "Bratcher?"

The attorney sealed the handshake. Firmer than Max

had expected. But Howard Bratcher quickly withdrew his hand to stand beside Rosie. "Yes. I'm Richard's brother. I know KCPD has reopened the investigation into his murder. Believe me, Detective, I'm as anxious as Rosemary to identify his killer and clear her name. Richard was an embarrassment to my father, and our law firm. There was no love lost between us. Rosemary's parents were clients of my father's, and she's been my friend and a client of the firm for several years. I'm here for her, not Richard."

Old family friends, hmm? Or something more? Howard slipped his arm behind Rosie's back, and her shoulders stiffened. Max's brewing suspicions edged into something more protective when she turned out of Bratcher's embrace and wound up facing the corner of the room. She reached out and brushed her fingertips across the back wall, and Max wondered if the word *trapped* was going through her mind again.

"Rosemary? I thought this might be a needlessly upsetting errand." Ah, hell. Was this guy thinking he could manipulate Rosie—and her money—the way his younger brother had? Despite his disclaimer, did Bratcher blame Rosie for his brother's murder and think she owed him some kind of payback? The solicitous attorney reached for her. "Would you like me to take you home?"

She wanted his protection? Max pulled out a chair and propped his foot on it, casually sitting back on the tabletop—purposefully blocking the attorney's path to Rosie. "She told you about the damage done to her house last night?"

The attorney pulled up short, his gaze dropping to the chair, then back up to Max. He was probably trying to figure out whether the lumbering detective was clueless, rude or smarter than he'd given him credit for. *That's right, buddy. It's the last one.* Howard Bratcher backed off a step and faced Max. "Yes. That's why I insisted on driving her here today."

Max's gaze went to the soft gray eyes that watched him from the corner of the room now. "Rosie's got her own car. She's perfectly capable of driving herself."

The attorney's eyes narrowed. "We've been close for several years, Detective. I'm concerned for her welfare."

How close? "Did you see the man who was taking pictures of her at the prison?"

"I didn't see anyone taking pictures."

Rosie stepped forward, grasping the back of the chair. "The man with the cell phone? I pointed him out to you. Described him as a lawyer-type guy?"

"I recall your amusing description, but—"

"You didn't stop to take a good look at the man who upset your close friend?" Max challenged.

"I don't remember."

Rosie's hopeful gaze crashed at Howard's noncommittal answer.

If this self-absorbed wise guy was her ally, no wonder she'd sought Max out for help. Even half-toasted, he'd paid attention to the details this bozo had missed. Unless Howie here had missed them on purpose. Could he be behind this terror campaign? Max's ability to read people might be on the fritz, but logic alone told him that a longtime friend would know best what kinds of things could frighten a woman the most.

For a split second, Max understood Rosie's aversion to being confined inside a small space. Especially with Mr. I'll-support-you-as-long-as-I'm-in-charge using up so much breathable air. With so-called friends like Bratcher here, Max wondered how much of Rosie's isolation had to do with her past, and how much had to do with her fear of getting *trapped* in another relationship with someone who, even without similar looks, had to remind her a lot of her dead ex-fiancé.

Following an instinct as ornery and strong as the urge to kiss her last night had been, Max snatched her hand, kicked the chair under the table and pulled her past the tailored suit. "Come with me, Rosie."

"Where are we going?"

He opened the door, picked up the mug shot books and tightened his grip around her protesting fingers as he led her into the familiar bustle of the main room.

Howard's snort of derision followed them out the door. "Shouldn't you address her as Miss March, Detective?"

Shouldn't you recuse yourself from serving as her attorney, Howie?

Max kept his snarky remark to himself and pulled Rosie around chairs and desks, colleagues and computer towers, suspects and complainants in for questioning and statements, until he reached the two desks pushed together where he and Trent worked. He dumped the notebooks on top of the blotter and pushed aside the mess of notes and files before pulling out his chair for her.

"It can get noisy out here, but you'll have plenty of space to spread out. Move anything you want that's in your way." She paused, tilting her face to his, no doubt questioning his sudden bout of chivalry—maybe even questioning if he was the same man she'd recruited for bodyguard duty last night. But the grief and guilt over Jimmy's death was firmly contained today. He hoped. Taking care of Rosie March—keeping her safe from stalkers and pompous attorneys and wannabe boyfriends—was his mission now. Flattening his hand at the small of her back, he urged her to sit. "I apologize for the clutter, but as you can see, there are no walls here. Those interview rooms are all tiny."

When her lips curved into a serene smile, Max nearly succumbed to the boyish urge to smile in return. "I can work here just fine. Thank you."

The crown of her hair brushed past his nose as she moved into the chair, and Max couldn't help but take a deep breath of her sweet, summery scent. A man could get addicted to Rosie's fragrance. Who was he kidding? Old maid bun and conservative clothes aside, Rosie March turned him on like some kind of crazy aphrodisiac. Maybe because he kept thinking of what she'd be like without the severe hairstyle and all that skin covered up.

Reminding himself that she was an assignment, and that she had more of a relationship with her dogs than she did with him, Max pulled the first mug shot book in front of her. "Here you go."

Her shoulders lifted with a resolute sigh and she flipped over the cover to look at the first six men. "So I just start turning pages to see if I recognize anyone who might have been watching me at the prison?"

"Or anywhere else. Unfortunately, we have even more photos you could look at, but I narrowed down the suspect pool to men with a history of harassment and other predatory crimes who fit the general description you gave." He left out the fact that pictures of Leland Asher and his known associates were scattered throughout the books, as well. If the crime boss was behind Richard Bratcher's murder or the threats against Rosie, she'd have to make the connection herself for any kind of case against him to stick. And if she recognized anyone who might be working for Howie here... Max tossed one of the books over to Trent's neat desk. "There, Howie. You can look through some of our pics, too. See if anyone there jogs your memory from the prison waiting room."

Not that he'd trust Bratcher's recognition, or lack thereof, of anyone in the book. But it would get the attorney farther out of Rosie's personal space.

Instead of taking the hint and moving to Trent's work space, Howard circled behind him to bookend the other side of Rosie's chair. "I don't like your tone, Detective Krolikowski. And I'd appreciate it if you'd show my client more respect."

"I've got nothing but respect for Miss March." Max leaned his hip against the edge of the desk, facing the woman between them. She was picking up the papers of an old report that had fanned across the desk and tucking them into a neat stack. "You got a key for me?" Max asked.

Howard put a hand on Rosie's shoulder. "What's he talking about?"

"This is between the lady and me." Although the dots of color on her cheeks made him wonder if she was going to renege on the deal they'd made. "Rosie? Do you remember my terms?"

Do what I say. When I say it. Trust me. If Jimmy had trusted him enough to share how bad things really were, then maybe Max could have gotten him help. He could have been there for his friend. He could have taken the gun away from him. He could have saved—

"I haven't forgotten." Rosie interrupted the guilty gloom of his thoughts and set aside the neat stack of papers before reaching into her purse. She pulled out a single key and laid it in his outstretched palm. Her fingers lingered a little longer, dotting his skin with warmth. Her upturned gaze locked on to his for a moment, as if she sensed that he'd checked out for a split second. "This was Stephen's. It will get you in the back entrance."

With Rosie unexpectedly pulling him back to the present, Max frowned, curling the key into his palm, catching her fingers in a quick squeeze before she drew away. "Not the main part of the house? Do I at least get access codes?"

The heat faded from her cheeks. "The apartment has a separate entrance. It's not hooked up to the alarm system. I didn't think you'd—"

"We'll make it work," Max interrupted when he saw Howard Bratcher leaning in to intervene. "I'll see you there on my lunch break."

"So soon?"

"I'm a soldier, remember? I travel light."

Howie's hand settled on her shoulder. "Rosemary, what is this detective talking about?"

Max stood to face him, squaring off over the top of Rosie's coppery bun. "Didn't she tell ya? We're moving in together."

"Excuse me?" Uh-huh. The touching? The temper? This guy thought he and Rosie were more than friends. He at least thought he could control her actions and influence her decisions.

Shrugging off her attorney's hand, Rosie went to work pulling items from beneath the three mug shot books and straightening the rest of his desk. "Max is moving into my downstairs apartment."

"That's right, Howie. I'm her new tenant." He had his story all worked out. "Good part of town. Use of a pool. My building is being renovated. Renting a couple of rooms costs less than staying in a hotel. And Rosie didn't seem to mind having a little extra security around the house."

"I see. Why didn't you tell me you were taking on a new tenant?"

Rosie's busy hands stopped. "Because it didn't concern you. My name has been in the papers, Howard. You said it yourself. *Kansas City's newest millionaire?* And now these threats?" She tilted her face up to her attorney. "Even with the security system you had me install, I've never really felt safe being there by myself. Duchess is getting older. Trixie makes a lot of noise but isn't a real threat to anyone. I really didn't think having a cop on the premises at night could hurt."

Howard knelt down beside the chair, pulling Rosie's hand into his. "You know I have connections to private security firms across the city. I could have hired someone if I'd known how truly frightened you were."

"I did tell you. I told Detective Krolikowski, too." She pulled her hand away and glanced over at Max before busying her hands again. "He listened."

Tell him, honey. Rosie March isn't alone and vulnerable anymore.

Howard pushed to his feet. That was not a friendly look. "You know I have only your best interests at heart, Rosemary."

"I know," Rosie answered. "And I'm grateful for all you've done for me. But I need to do this for myself. I need to do more to make decisions and handle my own problems."

"I see."

"Maybe you should go back to your office, Bratcher," Max suggested. "This may take a while. I can give Rosie a ride home. After all, we're heading to the same place."

"I'll be keeping an eye on you, Krolikowski. If you take advantage of Rosemary in any way, I will have your badge. And know I'll be asking around to find out what kind of cop you really are."

"Detective?" a quivering voice asked.

Max propped his hands at his waist, ready to take whatever threat this blowhard threw at him. "I intend to make sure no one takes advantage of her in any way."

"If you're using Rosemary as some kind of pawn in your investigation—"

"Max."

Rosie's sharp voice demanded his attention. "What is it?"

He braced a palm on the desk and leaned in to see what had alarmed her.

She held a picture that had fallen out of his file on Leland Asher. A picture of Asher and his entourage from a hoity-toity society event at the Nelson-Atkins Museum of Art. Only, Rosie wasn't pointing to the crime boss. She was pointing to the younger, shorter man with glasses standing on the other side of Asher's date.

"I know him. This is the man from the prison."

Chapter Eight

Rosemary wondered how she was ever going to survive the first night with Max Krolikowski living in her basement.

If she couldn't stop this restless pacing, flitting from one room to the next, she'd never get any sleep. She'd start a project in the library, leave it at the first unfamiliar noise and wind up in the kitchen, refreshing the dogs' water bowls. She'd hear the muffled voices of a television newscast through the floorboards, then head off to the front room to adjust the blinds. She'd peek out a window to look at the clouds gathering in the sky and covering the moon, but she'd hear the rumble of thunder in the distance and go back to the kitchen to make sure it was Mother Nature talking and not her new tenant grumbling about something downstairs. Then the dogs would woof at something outside and the whole anxious cycle would start over again.

Max's Cold Case Squad hadn't been able to immediately identify the man in the picture with Leland Asher, since he didn't have a record and wasn't in their criminal database. But she was certain the narrow-framed glasses and nondescript brown hair belonged to the man who'd smiled and taken her picture at the penitentiary. Knowing there was a mystery man out there somewhere, bent on terrorizing her, who might or might not have some connection to organized crime, was upsetting enough. But adding in the disruption of having a man on the premises once again, a man who seemed to occupy her thoughts the way Max did, left her unable to find any sense of calm or control. Routine, and the secure normalcy that went with it, had flown out the window.

Max had probably only needed a few minutes to put away the items he'd brought in his backpack and duffel bag and familiarize himself with the bedroom, bathroom and kitchenette, which he said would serve him just fine. And why wouldn't the man just go to bed already? One time she'd discovered Max out front, installing the new glass globes on her porch lights.

"The weatherman says we're having thunderstorms tonight," she warned.

"I know." He continued his work, sounding far too nonchalant about making himself at home here. "I want to make sure everything is secure before I head to bed." He nodded for her to go back inside. "But you go ahead."

Much later, she peeked out the door to find him reclining in her rocking chair, sitting in the dark with his big booted feet crossed on the porch railing. His shirt hung unbuttoned and loose from his shoulders, the tails flapping in the breeze that was picking up as lightning flashed in the clouds overhead. He still wore his gun and badge on his belt, and a stubby, unlit cigar that made him look like the gruff Army sergeant he'd once been was tucked into the corner of his mouth.

"Go to sleep, Rosie," he'd ordered, before removing the cigar and turning those watchful blue eyes to catch her spying on him. "You're safe."

Safe from her stalker, maybe. There'd been no phone call, no threat, no visit from anyone who wanted to hurt her for twenty-four hours now. But she wasn't so safe from the curious attraction she felt toward the unrefined yet inarguably masculine detective. And she certainly wasn't safe from the troubling memories of being alone with another man who'd turned her home into a prison where he'd inflicted pain and fear until fate alone had allowed her to escape.

"You won't bring that cigar into the house, will you?"

"No, ma'am."

Her fingers curled and uncurled around the edge of the door. "You need your sleep, too."

"Good night, Rosie."

Rosemary locked herself in her bedroom after that, counting down the hour until she heard the apartment door open and close at the back of the house. Duchess sat up from her cozy pillow beside Rosemary's bed, and Trixie yipped at the unfamiliar sound.

Lightning flashed and thunder rattled the window panes. A few seconds later the rain poured down, whipping through the trees and drumming on the new roof, finally drowning out the sounds of the house and the man in the room below hers.

"Settle down, girls," she whispered. "It's just a storm." The dogs curled into their respective beds and fell asleep long before Rosie turned out the bedside lamp and crawled beneath the sheet and quilt.

But it was hard to follow her own admonishment. Normally, the sounds of a summer storm lulled her into relaxing, but her sleep was disrupted by memories of the moonlight gleaming through the golden hair that dusted Max's muscular chest, and the desire to run her fingers there to discover the heat only hinted at when she'd touched him through his shirt. She remembered that kiss, too, and the way his hands had moved with such urgency through her hair. Maybe he'd put his hands in other places, skim them over her skin and pull her against all that brawny strength and heat. Maybe he'd kiss her again, and this time he wouldn't hold back. Maybe she wouldn't hold back, either.

Later, the bold wishes that filled her dreams and left her perspiring and uncomfortable in her crisp cotton sheets mutated into darker, more disturbing images.

Max's tawny jaw and imposing shoulders gave way to a shadow that was taller, slimmer, darker than the night. Rosemary squirmed in the tangle of covers as the shadow darted past her window. The black figure swirled around the walls of her bedroom, spinning closer, moving so fast that the sea of black miasma soon surrounded her bed. She moaned in her sleep as the blackness closed in all around her, stealing away the light, robbing her of warmth.

Her breathing quickened as the chill permeated her skin. But her arm was too weak to push it away. The darkness consumed her, reached right into her very heart and ripped it from her chest. Then she was burning, bleeding, begging for a reprieve.

A tiny circle of light flared in the darkness and a voice laughed. The tiny light was a fire, glowing brighter, hotter with every breath. She was powerless to move, powerless to do anything but anticipate the coming pain. Laughter rang through the darkness as the fire moved closer and closer, until the hot ember hissed against her cold skin, branding her.

Rosemary came awake screaming. She shot up in bed, her hand clutching at the scars on her collarbone, her heart pounding in her chest. In the instant she realized the torture had been a dream, the instant she realized the shadows were no more than one of the Dinkles' trees, silhouetted by lightning against her window shade, the instant she realized she was perfectly fine and lowered her hand, she realized the laughter was real. High-pitched. Distorted. Distant.

The threat was real.

Duchess was on her feet, growling at the window. Trixie jumped onto the bed and barked. The repetitive laughter, fading in and out like a clown running in circles, was coming from outside in the storm.

"Max?" Fear hammered her pulse in her ears. She needed Max.

A clap of thunder slammed like a door in the distance, and Rosemary jumped inside her skin. "Rosie?" She heard a rapid knocking, like gunshots at her back door. "Rosie!"

"Max?" Rosemary quickly kicked away the covers twisted around her legs and slid off the edge of the bed. She pulled her sleep shirt down to her thighs and crossed to the door. "I'm coming!" But the laughter started up again behind her and she froze. It grew louder, tinnier. The knocking at her back door stopped and a chill skittered down her spine.

Grabbing Duchess's collar as she walked past, Rosemary went to the window. With her heart in her throat, she pulled back the curtain and peeked between the shade and the sill. Lightning flashed and she jumped back from the faceless figure in a black hood standing there.

She screamed again.

A deeper voice shouted outside in the storm. "KCPD! Get on the ground!" The laughter stopped abruptly and when the next bolt of lightning flashed, her window was empty. She saw a blur of movement in the blowing rain as she dropped the curtain and backed away. She heard a familiar grumble of curses.

"Max!" she shouted. What was he doing? If the intruder could threaten her dogs and terrorize her, what would he do to Max? What if he bashed in Max's head with that baseball bat? Would he kill the detective guarding her? Then who would stop him from coming after her? Saving Max was imperative to saving herself. Saving Max was imperative, period. "Max?" Tripping over the excited barking dogs, Rosemary turned and ran. Her fingers fumbled with the stupid lock on her door before she finally opened the thing and slung it open. "Max!"

The wood floor was cold beneath her bare feet, the kitchen tile even colder. She ran through the darkened house but skidded to a stop and abruptly changed course at the furious sound of knocking at her front door now. "Rosie!" He was safe. She would be safe. "Open the damn door! Rosie! Answer me!"

"I'm here. Is he out there? Did you catch him?"

"Rosie!"

She punched in the alarm code, unhooked the chain and dead bolt, turned the knob. Max jerked the storm door from her grasp the moment she'd turned its lock. The blowing rain whooshed in sideways around him, splashing her face and shirt before he pushed her back inside the foyer.

"You've got too many damn locks. I couldn't get to you." While he griped away, she ran straight into his arms, pressing her cheek against the wet skin of his chest, sliding her hands beneath his soggy shirttails and linking them together at the back of his waist. He walked her back another couple of steps, shutting the steel door behind him. "I lost him. You have to answer me when I call you. You can't scream like that and not answer…

Okay." Once the adrenaline was out of his system, once he realized how she shuddered against him, clinging tightly to his strength and heat, he curled one arm behind her back and set his gun on the front hall table with the other. His growly tone softened. "Okay, honey." He reached behind him to throw the bolt yet never let go. Then he came back to wrap both arms around her and nestle his jaw at the crown of her hair. She willingly rocked back and forth as his chest expanded and contracted against her after the exertion of chasing a shadow through the storm. "I'm gettin' you all wet."

She shook her head against the strong beat of his heart. "I don't care."

He pulled her sleep-tossed hair from the neckline of her pink T-shirt, smoothing it down her back in gentle strokes. "You're okay. He's gone."

"Did he hurt you?" A crisp wet curl of chest hair tickled her lips. A muscle quivered beneath the unintended caress.

"Me? Nah, I'm too tough for that kind of thing. Are *you* hurt?" He sifted his fingers through her hair until his warm, callous palm cupped the nape of her neck. "Ah, hell, honey. Your skin's like ice." He shifted his stance then, curling his shoulders around her, rubbing his hands up and down her back. "I heard a noise and saw that guy outside your window, but I lost him in the rain once he jumped the Dinkles' hedge out front. And it's way too dark to be firing blindly into shadows. I didn't want to take the time away from you to do a search, in case he doubled back and broke in. I couldn't risk leaving you alone."

Rosemary's shirt and panties were slowly soaking up the moisture from his rain-soaked clothes. But the furnace of heat on the other side of those wet jeans and unbuttoned shirt that he must have hastily tossed on seeped right through the layers of damp material, warming her skin and easing her panic.

Once they were both breathing normally again, he pressed his lips against her temple before easing some space between them, although he continued rubbing his hands up and down her back and the arms she crossed between them. "Tell me what happened."

She watched the rain from his scalp run in rivulets down to his scruffy jaw, pooling at the tip of his chin before dripping onto her arm. "I had a nightmare."

His hands stopped their massage and squeezed her shoulders, demanding she meet his concerned gaze. "Uh-uh. That guy was real. Standard-issue hoodie and dark jeans. At least six feet tall. Wish I'd taken the time to grab my flashlight so I could have seen his face."

The cop was returning. The warmth was leaving. Rosemary hugged her arms more tightly around her waist, suddenly self-conscious to be standing toes to toes in a puddle in her foyer wearing little more than her long pink T-shirt. A wet T-shirt now. Not that she had any illusions about turning Max's head, but she didn't want to embarrass him, either. "I was dreaming of things Richard did to me. When I woke up, that man was at my window. For a split second, I thought..." She shrugged away from Max's touch and shivered. "It was the same man who vandalized my porch. I'm sure of it."

"Your scream woke me. When I got outside, I heard that crazy caterwauling." He picked up his gun and tucked it into the back of his jeans before scrubbing his fingers over his chin and wiping the moisture on the front of his shirt. Was she really still standing there, staring at the glistening wet skin of his chest? "Sorry," he apologized, mistaking her fascinated longing for some kind of effrontery. His big fingers fumbled to pull the soggy cotton together over the hills and hollows of muscle and hook a few buttons to the placket. "He's long gone. There were footprints beneath the sill. I went back to snap a picture, but they're washing away." Max reached into his shirt pocket and pulled out a little red plastic box. "I found this out there in the grass." He pushed a button, and a warped recording of laughter played.

Rosemary recoiled from the sound. "That's what I heard."

"It's cheap. A noisemaker from a party store. Sounds as though there's water in the mechanism. With the storm, there's no way we're getting fingerprints off this thing. Maybe on the inside, though. Looks like there's something wedged in there. Do you have a plastic bag?" Although she missed the warmth of his body pressed against hers, she knew this businesslike interchange was more important than her own foolish cravings for physical contact. Tucking her hair behind her ears, she nodded. The dogs fell into step beside her, joining their little parade to the kitchen. Max brought up the rear, stopping in each doorway along the hall, checking inside the rooms to make sure everything was still secure. "Sorry about your floor. I'm making a mess."

She stopped at the bathroom to pull her robe from behind the door and shrugged into it, adding another layer of warmth and modesty now that she was done throwing herself at her downstairs tenant. "It'll clean up. I believe you think I'm a prim-and-proper prude. A little mud and water don't bother me." Stepping into the kitchen, Rosemary flipped on the light and eyed the path of water and big muddy prints from Max's bare feet that marked her hallway. "The dogs have tracked in worse. I just like knowing the rules and what's expected of me—

and what to expect from other people." She crossed to the bank of drawers beside the oven but hesitated. "I hope I didn't put you in an awkward position before. I don't normally wrap myself around a man while I'm in my pajamas." The burn of embarrassment crept up her neck and into her cheeks at that rather suggestive description of seeking refuge in his arms. "I mean, I don't…not without asking first. But I was scared. And I was worried about you."

Rosemary glanced up as he leaned his hip against the countertop beside her. "Do you hear me complaining?"

She was relieved, and more disappointed than she should be, to see him dismissing her panicked indiscretion with a wry grin. She tried to match his easy smile. "You *are* very good at vocalizing what you're thinking and feeling, aren't you, Detective?"

His smile disappeared and he reached over to catch a tendril of hair that stuck to her damp cheek and tucked it behind her ear. "I thought I'd earned a Max from you by now."

Her gaze drifted to the front of his shirt and the three buttons that he'd fastened into the wrong holes. Rosemary couldn't stop the smile from curving her lips again. This man was a tornado blowing through her controlled, predictable world, upsetting her routine, ignoring her personal barriers, waking wants and needs she thought had died long ago. And yet he was growing more dear to her, more necessary as a protector, a friend and maybe something more, with each encounter. Even if all he ever wanted from her was a drunken kiss and the chance to solve Richard's murder, she was glad that he'd barged into her closed-off, humdrum life. She opened a drawer and pulled out a box of plastic storage bags for him. "Here. Max."

Nodding his approval, Max pulled a pocketknife from the front of his jeans to pry open the red box. "Looks like our perp took it apart to modify it somehow. Even with industrial glue, though, it didn't reseal completely. That's probably how the water got inside."

"That horrible sound reminded me of Richard. Of that night. He laughed when he…" The scars on her chest seem to throb and she tied the robe more snugly around her damp T-shirt.

"Who would know about him laughing that night?" Max asked, pulling out a chair at the table to tinker with the box. "Somebody had to know it would rattle you."

"I'm not sure. It's probably in the police report."

"That's public record if somebody looks hard enough. Who else?"

Rosemary considered herself a very private person, but after that night, she'd been desperate to find someone who could help her escape Richard's tyranny. "My brother, Stephen. A couple of friends."

"What friends?" Max glanced up from unscrewing the back of the box. "Crimes are solved in the details. I need you to tell them to me."

Rosemary wondered if the storm outside could somehow cool the air inside the house, as well. "Otis and Arlene, when I went to their house to call the police afterward. Howard."

"Your attorney?"

She nodded. "I told him everything when he was putting together the restraining order."

What about a statuesque blonde who blamed her for Richard's death?

"You got a suspect for me?" he prompted, sensing her thoughts turning.

Rosemary pulled out another chair and sat kitty-corner from him. "Richard could have told one of his mistresses. I ran into one of them at Howard's office the other day."

"*One* of…?" Max's curse was short and pungent. "Sorry. I know you hate that."

"Not as much as I hate not knowing who's doing this to me. Her name is Charleen Grimes. She said your friends Detectives Watson and Parker had shown up at her boutique to ask her questions. She was pretty ticked off." Rosemary remembered the hate and pain spewing from Charleen's perfectly painted lips that day. "She accused me of killing Richard."

"And getting away with it? Like that first note?"

Rosemary nodded. Charleen's verbal attack in Howard's office that day still rankled. But the memory of the blonde woman striding across Howard's office and towering over her was triggering a different memory. "Charleen is tall for a woman. Could she pass for a man at night, in the shadows?"

"It's possible. The guy I chased tonight was wearing clothes so baggy and nondescript I'd be hard-pressed to confirm a gender. I just assumed it was a guy." He wedged the tip of his pocketknife into the seam around the box. "I want to meet this Charleen… Finally." With one more twist of his knife, the box popped open and a soggy piece of paper fell out and plopped to the floor.

"What's that?"

He put out a hand to keep her from picking it up. "Don't touch it. I'll bag it for prints and have Trent take it to the lab tomorrow."

"You know it's not there by accident. I want to know what it says."

He used the plastic bag to retrieve it from the floor and gently shake it open. "Ah, hell."

It was a black-and-white photocopy of a picture. Of her.

Her thoughts instantly went to the mysterious photographer who'd snapped a picture of her in the visitors' room at the state prison. It was even more disturbing to see her wearing a different outfit than the flowered blouse she'd worn that day. She didn't have to move any closer to see the candid image of her climbing into a cab outside Howard's office building. "How long has he been watching me?"

When Max would have slipped the note into the bag and hidden it away, she grabbed his wrist and insisted on seeing every last gruesome detail.

Her eyes and heart had been x-ed out on the picture. Someone who was very angry with her had drawn a noose around her neck in black ink and typed a message neatly across the top.

I want to feel my hands around your throat, your pulse stopping beneath the pressure of my thumbs. You will burn for what you've done.

There will be justice for Richard.

Ha. Ha. Ha.

But the creepiest part was the five black marks dotting the top of the white dress she wore—five dots right across her collarbone where the burn scars Richard had inflicted upon her lay.

"How could he know? How could anyone know?"

Rosemary was only vaguely aware of Max moving as the room swirled around her. With her hand at her throat, she sank into the back of the chair and closed her eyes.

"Rosie?"

She heard the gruff voice calling to her in the distance. Someone knew her darkest secrets. Someone was using those secrets against her. To terrorize her. To punish her. To plunge her into a nightmare from which she could never escape.

"Rosie."

Rough hands grabbed her shoulders, shook her. She was cold. So cold.

Then the hands closed around either side of her head and she fell forward until her mouth ran into something firm, hot. Something warm and moist pressed between her lips, parting them. The world gradually took the shape and form of fingers tangled in her hair, tugging lightly at her scalp. The pressure on her mouth became pliant lips that tasted of salt and heat and toasty tobacco. The taste was familiar yet new. Potent, with a tickle of sandpapery stubble on the side. Max. Max was kissing her. His hands were holding her. His tongue was sliding against hers. In one moment, she was the stunned recipient of bold passion—in the next, her tongue darted out to catch his and she leaned into the kiss. Deepened it. Came alive with it. Her throat hummed with anticipation. She stretched to fit her mouth more fully against his.

But when her hands came to rest against his chest, he pulled away. The room was still swaying when her eyes fluttered open and she looked into the damp, craggy face of the man kneeling in front of her chair. "Max?"

He stroked his thumb across her tender lips, brushed her hair behind her ears. "You checked out on me there. Don't scare me like that, okay? Stay with me."

The disorienting fear and helplessness faded. Other emotions—confusion, hope, desire—grew stronger. She touched the lines of concern crinkling beside his eyes. She brushed her thumb across the masculine line of his bottom lip, absorbing the heat from his skin into hers.

She could hear her heart beating over the drumbeat of rain outside. "Another opportunity you couldn't pass up?" But there was no humor in her laugh, no answering humor in his eyes. "You shouldn't kiss me like that unless it means something to you."

Max's lip trembled beneath her thumb. A deep groan rose from his chest. And then he was pushing to his feet, pulling her with him. His mouth covered hers, hot and wet and full of a driving need she answered kiss for kiss.

He lifted her onto her toes and she wound her arms around his neck, leaning into his sheltering strength. There was little finesse to Max's kiss. But then, she had little to compare it to beyond Richard's smooth, practiced seduction that left her feeling unsatisfied and inadequate.

Rosemary liked this infinitely better. There was little to second-guess about a man sliding his hands down her back to squeeze her bottom and lift her off her feet into his hard thighs and the firm interest stirring in between. Max's cheek rasped against hers as his lips scudded across her jaw and pulled at her earlobe.

His words were basic. "Your skin's so soft. Your hair smells like summer and rain. It's the cleanest scent. I could breathe it in all night long."

When he reclaimed her lips, his tongue was bold, his hands were bolder. Rosemary gasped when she felt his palms branding her skin beneath her shirt. The tips of her breasts tingled, grew heavy and tight as they rubbed against the hard wall of his chest. She wanted his hands there, soothing their needy distress, exciting them more. This kiss was the wildest, most unexpected, most perfect embrace of her life. She was an equal partner, giving, taking. She slipped her hands up into the prickly crop of his military-short hair, turning his head to the angle of kiss she liked best.

"Rosie…honey…" His fingers dipped beneath the elastic of her panties. Yes. She wanted his touch there, too. She was forgetting the past. She was unafraid of the future. There was only Max and this moment and feeling safe and desired.

But when she curled her leg around Max's knee, instinctively opening herself to the need arcing between them, he pulled his lips away with a noisy moan. Her mouth chased after his to reclaim the connection, but his hands were on her shoulders now, pulling her arms from around his neck. Her toes touched the cold tile floor again, jarring her back to common sense. Suddenly, the water that had soaked through her clothes seemed just as cold. She rested her hands at his shoulders a moment to steady herself but curled her body away from his. One moment she was alive and on fire, the next, she was shivering and confused.

Rosemary grasped the back of the chair to keep herself standing as Max determinedly backed away. "That's not why I'm here. I've got a mission. I made a promise." His chest expanded with a deep, ragged breath. "Ah, hell. Quit looking at me like you either want to shoot me or eat me up. I'm trying to do the right thing here."

Max's rejection instantly sent her back to the times in her relationship with Richard when he'd rebuffed her advances. "I wasn't very good, was I? I'm sor—"

"Do *not* let that man come between us." Max swiped his hand over his mouth and jaw and spun away. Just as quickly he faced her again and grabbed her wrist. "You call me whatever crass SOB you want to." He pulled her hand to the front of his jeans and cupped it over the unmistakable warm bulge behind his zipper. "This is what you do to me. I don't know why you and me fit together this good. If I could take you to bed right now and finish this, I would." He released her and backed away, raising his hands in apology. "But that's not what I'm here for. Neither one of us needs that kind of complication in our lives. I have to keep the mission in mind. I'm a cop. I have to think like a cop, not a…"

"Not a what?" she asked, her voice barely a whisper.

But he didn't fill in the blank. "It's not your job to deal with me. I'm damaged goods, Rosie. You can do better than me."

"Now who's apologizing?"

With a shrug of his massive shoulders, he scooped up the noisemaker and message that had sent her into shock and slipped them into plastic bags. "I'm going back outside to give everything a once-over—make sure our friend hasn't come back. I need to call this in to my team, too. My description of the perp is pretty vague, but it's a place to start. I'll have a black-and-white swing through the neighborhood, just in case he's hiding out somewhere." He headed to the back door. "I'll be right downstairs. Just a scream away."

Rosemary shook off her stupor and ran after him, grabbing his arm. "You're leaving me?"

He looked down over the jut of his shoulder at her, his growly voice calming. "I don't want to push my luck by overstaying my welcome."

Right. He was being all noble, doing this for her, respecting the boundaries she'd forgotten herself. She released her desperate grasp and stepped away, rubbing her hands up and down her chilled arms. "You better go call your team. I'll be fine."

"You're gettin' pale again. I'll stay if you want me to."

Rosemary shook her head. "No. You have a job to do. I'll be fine. You're here for me to draw out Richard's killer, not to babysit me."

"You know that's not the only reason I'm here."

"For my dad? You said you owed something to a man like him."

Max exhaled a grumbling sigh. "I doubt your dad would make me ten kinds of crazy the way you do. Would you really be okay with me here in the house? Because, frankly, running up and down those basement stairs and breaking through all your locked doors makes me feel like I'm miles away. What if that guy wasn't content to stay outside your window? If he'd gotten inside the house I'd have had to shoot my way in to get to you."

She was so confused—coming to terms with the idea that she could have feelings and desire for a man again, wanting to solve Richard's murder as quickly as possible, evaluating the false boundaries of her reclusive life that had at least given her the illusion of being safe— what was she supposed to choose? "I don't think gunfire in the house would be safe for Duchess and Trixie."

"Or for you. Would you feel safer if I stayed tonight?"

"I don't know."

"Yeah, you do. Everything else aside, would you feel safer?" He tapped his cheek to ask her to look him in the eye and answer. "Up here, honey."

She did look up into those expectant blue eyes. Yes. In every way that mattered, she felt safe with Max. Rosemary nodded.

"Say it, Rosie. Don't make me think I'm bullying you into this."

"I'm not inviting you into my bed. But you are awfully warm, and I can't seem to shake this chill and..." She hugged her arms around her waist but bravely held his gaze. "I don't want to be alone tonight. Would you stay with me?"

The taut line of his mouth relaxed. "I like a clear set

of rules, too. So no hanky-panky, but you wouldn't be adverse to a little cuddling? You know, so I can keep an eye on you and you could borrow some body heat?"

"That would be enough for you?"

He brushed a copper tendril off her cheek and tucked it behind her ear. "That would be perfect."

Rosemary smiled. "Then I can live with those rules, too."

"You know the drill." He opened the door. The wind had shifted, blowing rain beneath the patio roof and through the screen, getting their damp clothes wet again. "Lock up. Keep the dogs with you."

"Yes, sir."

Max hurried over to the apartment entrance to make his phone calls and she locked the door behind him. Plucking the wet cotton knit away from the goose bumps on her skin, Rosemary whistled for the dogs. "Come on, girls."

She changed into a fresh sleep shirt and gathered a sponge and some towels, and dropped to her hands and knees to mop up the mud and water in the foyer and hallway. By the time Max returned, she had a load of soiled towels going in the laundry, the dogs settled in with rawhide treats and her quilt pulled off her bed to wrap around her shoulders as a makeshift robe until her own clothes dried.

Max toweled himself off and changed into a dry T-shirt and jeans he'd brought with him before wandering into the library to find her sitting on the rug, going through another box of her parents' things. He took a sip of the hot decaf coffee she'd fixed for him. "I'm willing to take the couch, but I've slept on enough hard bunks and sandy ground to want to avoid the floor if that's okay."

Rosemary grinned and pointed to the sofa where

Trixie had climbed on top of the pillow and blanket she'd set out for Max. "Just push her off. She's got plenty of rugs and pillows around the house to sleep on."

While she finished sorting through an envelope of photographs from a family vacation, tossing the blurry pictures and duplicates in the trash, Max sat. Instead of jumping down, Trixie climbed into his lap and lifted her paws for a thorough tummy rub. When Duchess abandoned her treat and came over to share a little bit of the action, Max reached down to rub the German shepherd's tummy, too.

But then he clapped his hands and shooed both dogs away to turn his full attention on Rosemary. "It's late. We have meetings tomorrow, a couple of leads I'd like to pursue. And in case you thought it was up for debate, it's not—you're coming with me."

When she reached for another envelope of photographs, Max cleared his throat. "Honey, you need some sleep. So do I. Either go to bed or come here."

The teasing command overrode any shyness or second thoughts she was feeling. Clutching the quilt around her shoulders, Rosemary turned off the desk lamp. Max turned off the lamp beside the sofa and set his gun and badge on the table beside his coffee mug. Rosemary sat down beside him, watching the diminishing lightning flicker through the blinds in the front window.

A voice, equally dark as the room now, spoke beside her. "The rules I agreed to included some cuddling." He draped his arm over the back of the couch behind her shoulders, reminding her of the body heat she craved. She curled her feet beneath the quilt beside her and leaned into him, resting her head against his shoulder. His arms folded around her and the quilt, tucking them both to his side. "That's better."

Without a visible clock to keep track of the time, she wasn't sure how long it was before the warmth of the quilt and man holding her seeped deep into her bones and she was drifting off to sleep. "Max?"

"Hmm?"

"You called me honey tonight. More than once."

"I guess it just slipped out. I wasn't trying to over-step—"

"I like it. I like that you call me Rosie, too. Nobody else calls me Rosie. It makes me feel…normal."

"Normal?"

"You know, not an unemployed millionaire murder suspect who talks to her dogs more than she does to people?" She rested her palm above the deep-pitched chuckle that vibrated his chest. "I'm sorry to be so much trouble. I'm glad you're here. But if I wig out on you at some point during the night, just know it's nothing personal."

"Uh-uh." Max slipped his fingers under her chin and tilted her face to his. "You don't apologize for anything. Whatever you have to say to me, don't be afraid to say it. I'm not Richard. What you see is what you get. You know what I'm thinking or feeling at almost any given moment. It isn't always pretty, but there are no surprises."

"I don't like surprises, anyway."

"You, lady, are the biggest surprise of all." He pressed a chaste kiss to her forehead before swinging his legs up onto the couch and stretching out beside her, pulling the quilt up over them both. "Now, go to sleep. That's an order."

Feeling toastier and more tired by the second, Rosie curled up against Max and drifted off to a deep, nightmare-free sleep.

MAX AWOKE TO sunlight streaming through the blinds, a dog licking his elbow and feeling incredibly hard.

He supposed a creamy thigh wedged between his legs did that to a man. And while there might have been a woman in his past he'd have undressed and gotten busy with to start the new day, this was Rosie March. And there were rules with Rosie. Keeping her safe, proving her innocence, earning her trust and fighting to make sure he was worthy of whatever affection she threw his way meant following those rules as surely as he'd follow an order from a superior officer. Still, while she snored softly on his chest, he raised his head and breathed in the sweet, clean scent of her copper-red hair that reminded him of coming home and leaving battlefields behind him. He wasn't a saint, after all.

But a bigger pair of deep brown eyes were staring at him now. Between Duchess's stoic plea and Trixie's eager tongue rasping along his arm, Max got the message. He reached down to scratch around the poodle's ears. "Need to go outside, girls?"

When Duchess jumped to her feet and the little dog started dancing around, Max tried to calm them. "Shh. Mama's sleeping. I'm coming. Give me a sec."

Sometime during the night, the quilt had ended up on the floor, and Trixie had claimed it for a bed, so there was nothing but the woman herself he needed to extricate himself from. Max palmed Rosie's hip and gently lifted her so he could pull his legs from beneath hers. Then he turned onto his side to pull his shoulder from beneath her head. But his efforts to carefully free himself from the woman draped on top of him without waking or embarrassing her halted when the neckline of her T-shirt gaped open and he shamelessly took a peek at the plump, heavy breasts that had pillowed against his side and chest most of the night.

But that little rush of lust quickly dissipated when he saw the puckery burn scars along her collarbone, marring Rosie's beautiful skin. He tucked his finger beneath the stretchy cotton and pulled the material aside to get a better look.

"Son of a…" Five perfect white circles the size of a cigarette tip. That explained the high necklines. He dropped his knees to the floor and pulled his arm away as his temper brewed. He vowed then and there to give up the cigars completely—not even a stress-relieving chomp for old times' sake. Nobody did that kind of damage to themselves. That was done to her. He'd have been tempted to pull the trigger on Richard Bratcher himself if he'd known that bastard had trapped her inside the house and tortured her like that.

Jimmy had been tortured. Physically, mentally, emotionally. Had Rosie endured the same?

Jimmy hadn't survived the aftermath of all that had been done to him, all he'd seen. In the end, he'd died alone. If there'd been anything in Max's power he could do to save his buddy, he would have.

Rosie was all alone in this house. But she wasn't going to cope with Bratcher and his cruelty by herself anymore. For Rosie, for her father, for his own sanity and redemption, Max intended to capture a killer and put a stop to anyone or anything that tried to hurt this woman again.

Perhaps sensing his unblinking stare and darkening mood, Rosie stirred on the couch. She smiled before opening her eyes. "Good morning."

Max didn't trust himself to speak. He curled his fingers into a fist and pulled it away from her.

Rosie's smile disappeared in an instant and she was wide-awake. When she saw the direction of his gaze, she sat up and scooted to the far end of the couch. "What are you doing?"

"Trying not to put a fist through your wall."

"Ugly, aren't they?" She pulled her oversize shirt back into its modest place and picked up the quilt, draping it over her shoulders and covering everything between her chin and her feet. "I suppose with nine million dollars, I could afford to get some plastic surgery and make them disappear. They're there to remind me that I've never really been safe, I've never really been free since that man entered my life. I can never drop my guard or give my heart again. Not until the rumors are put to rest and that crazy stalker—"

When she pushed to her feet, Max was there to stop her from bolting from the room. He caught her face between his hands and dipped his head to kiss her. It was brief, it was passionate, it was full of the unspoken promise he'd made to her moments earlier.

When he released her, she wasn't quite so set on running from him. "What was that for?"

"I saw the chance to do it, so I did."

Shaking off his show of support, his vow to protect her, she headed for the hall anyway. "I don't think I can do this, after all, Max. You need to go."

"Did Bratcher put those marks on you?"

She stopped, pulling the quilt more fully around her. Her huddled silence was answer enough. Hell. No wonder she'd checked out last night when she saw that sick, doctored-up picture. That kind of graphic accuracy about her past abuse had no other function but to remind her of her worst fears. To make her feel as powerless and alone now as she had back then.

He wasn't giving Rosie the chance to ever feel that way again. "Shower and get dressed and grab some breakfast—or whatever your morning routine is. You're coming with me today."

"But you have to work." Her shoulders lifted with a heavy sigh and she turned, gesturing to the boxes and books all around them. "And I'm still going through Mom and Dad's papers. You don't think I'm safe here during the day? I'll have Duchess and Trixie with me. Send one of your uniformed officers over to keep an eye on me." She shrugged the quilt higher onto her shoulders and hugged it tight around her neck, hiding even more of herself from him—as if his body hadn't already memorized the shape and weight of those generous hips and breasts. "Won't I just be in the way?"

"You aren't a prisoner in this house anymore, Rosie. We talked about this last night. Staying here by yourself isn't an option. I don't want to wait until Trent or someone else from the team gets done with morning roll call to take over the watch here—and I won't trust you with anyone else. We have secrets to uncover, a murder to solve."

"And you think I can help?"

"This morning I have a meeting at Endicott Global. I'd like you to come along on the off chance we see your guy from the picture, or anyone else you might recognize there. In fact, I want you to keep your eyes open anyplace we go, in case he's following you." KCPD still hadn't identified the young man yet. But Max had a feeling in his gut that the man was key to linking Bratcher's murder to Leland Asher's organization and a host of other crimes. "Before we do that, we're going next door. Your neighbors are always peeking at you and seem to have an opinion on everything. Maybe they saw something last night."

"Oh, joy."

Good. Sarcasm beat that self-conscious guilt and avoiding him. "You're the key to my investigation, Rosie. Maybe the key to my redemption over Jimmy's death, too."

"That wasn't your fault."

He put up a hand to stop that argument. "You fight your demons your way, and I'll deal with mine on my own terms. I want you in my sights 24/7 now. Okay? I promise to knock off at five when my shift is over, and I'll bring you back to do your paperwork thing here."

"You're not really giving me a choice, are you?"

"If you don't go, neither do I. And that means we'll never find Bratcher's killer."

A beat of silence passed before she nodded and turned. "Put the dogs in the backyard on your way out. I'll get ready."

Chapter Nine

"Brace yourself," Max warned, pressing the doorbell. "And remember, the idea is to keep them talking."

Rosemary inhaled a steadying breath and hugged her shoulder bag closer to the navy blue animal-print dress she wore. "That shouldn't be hard."

Arlene Dinkle wasn't smiling when she answered the front door. But then, neither was Max.

With a clean shave and a fresh shirt tucked into his jeans, there was little left of the man who'd held Rosemary so tenderly and securely through the night. This guy wore a gun and a badge and an attitude that outgrumped Arlene's early-morning mood.

"Good morning, Mrs. Dinkle." Max flashed his badge but not a smile. "You remember me, don't you?"

"Detective Krolikowski." Arlene carried pruning shears and a small bouquet of cut roses in her gloved hands. "I remember you. Did you catch that trespasser?"

"The department's working on it. I'm following up on what might be a related crime. There was an attempted break-in at Miss March's house last night, and I was wondering if you or your husband saw anything. May we come in?"

"Strange men at all hours, that old car parked in your driveway, and now this?" Arlene's dark gaze slid over to

Rosemary. "You draw a bad element to this neighborhood like a magnet, don't you?"

Bristling at the catty remark, Max's hand clenched at the small of Rosemary's back. But his tone remained good-ol'-boy professional. "Let's get one thing straight, Mrs. Dinkle. You do not get to speak to Miss March like that. She's a victim, not a criminal. You'll give her the same respect you would this badge."

The older woman's petite frame puffed up. "Well, I've never been spoken to—"

"Rosemary. Good morning." Otis strolled out of the kitchen in a pair of track pants and a muscle shirt, carrying a ball cap and bottle of water. He reached around his wife to push open the screen door. "Detective. Please, come in."

There was no offer of a cup of coffee, not even an offer to sit. The fragrance from the roses Arlene had been trimming overwhelmed their small foyer and tickled Rosemary's sinuses. But Otis's welcoming smile seemed genuine. "Trouble next door again?"

"I'm afraid so, sir."

"A man peeked in my window last night," Rosemary explained, trying to keep her tone as even and uncowed by Arlene's rudeness as Max's had been. "He left a threat that indicated he wanted to kill me."

"Oh, my. That's terrible." Otis's smile faded. He swung his gaze over to Max. "Did you catch him?"

"The police haven't caught anybody," Arlene groused. "Now we have Peeping Toms making death threats running around our neighborhood? You know if they can't get into your house, Rosemary, they'll try to break into ours." She thumped her husband's arm. "We can't afford the same kind of high-tech security she has. I told you we should have sold this house and moved ten years ago." She swung her arms out, indicating the rest of the house, inadvertently drawing Rosemary's attention to at least five more vases of roses scattered across the living room. "You never listen."

"Is there a flower show coming up, Arlene?" Rosemary asked. The woman certainly loved her gardening, but the overwhelming smell of attar in the house was giving her a bit of a headache.

"I'm trying to save my prize roses," Arlene explained. "That storm last night nearly did them in. At least I can dry these and save the perfume for potpourri. Unless, of course, some gang person breaks in and robs us. Or kills us in our sleep."

"We're perfectly fine here, Arlene." Otis's quiet, almost monotonous voice was such a contrast to his wife's shrill tones. "Rosemary's the one who's been hurt, not you. It was probably some crackpot who wanted to see what a millionaire looks like."

"Or someone casing the homes in the neighborhood to rob us," she insisted. "I told you about that fancy truck I've seen cruising up and down the street at all hours of the night. And don't think I haven't asked. No one around here owns it."

Otis shrugged. "I would have heard anyone poking at our windows. The game was on until one in the morning." He scratched the bald spot on top of his head. "Now that I think of it, I did hear some shouting last night. I figured it was someone caught out in the storm."

Arlene clutched the roses to her chest. "They were probably sending signals, telling each other how to get in. Otis, you should have called the police."

"Why? I couldn't make out any words."

Max held up a hand to end the marital debate. "It was

probably me shouting. The perp never said a word. Could you tell me a little more about this 'fancy truck,' ma'am?"

The woman could certainly be counted on for details. "I don't know models and makes, but it was one of those extended cab trucks, with a backseat for passengers?" Max pulled a pen and notebook from his pocket and jotted the description. "It was dark green—almost looked black, but I saw it under the street lamp a couple of nights ago and it was definitely dark green. The trim around the wheel wells was black, though."

"Did you happen to get a license plate?"

She thought for a moment. "I don't think it had one. It had those stickers in the window—the ones the dealer puts on when you first buy a car?"

"That helps."

Arlene almost smiled at the morsel of praise.

But her sour frown returned when Otis reached out and patted Rosemary's shoulder. "Are you all right, dear?"

She nodded. "But understandably, seeing the man gave me a good scare. I'm lucky Max was there."

Arlene crossed her arms with a noisy harrumph. "Your parents would have been mortified to know you're alone in their house entertaining a man overnight."

Her parents would have been glad to know that Max had kept her safe. "Not that it's any of your business, Arlene, but Max is renting Stephen's old apartment downstairs."

"Oh." That seemed to deflate Arlene's judgmental superiority a bit. "I misunderstood. So the police are providing extra protection for dangerous neighborhoods like ours?"

The only danger zone on this block seemed to be Rosemary's house. But until she could prove her innocence, she supposed Arlene would continue to believe she lived next door to a murderess and a hive for illegal activities. "It's nice to have a cop living nearby, isn't it?" Rosemary choked out the polite words in the name of neighborhood peace and getting the Dinkles to answer Max's questions.

Max didn't waste time with making nice. "Did you see the green truck last night, ma'am?"

Arlene pursed her lips together, thinking. "No."

"When the truck was here before, did you happen to look at the driver?"

"Not really."

"Did either of you see or hear anything around midnight last night?" Max asked.

Otis crossed his arms and shrugged. "We had that big thunderstorm blow through about that time. Pretty noisy. I didn't hear anything."

"But you were awake watching the ball game?" Max clarified. "I pursued the suspect in the direction of your yard. He crashed through the hedge out front and took off between the houses. I lost him in the storm."

"My hawthorn bushes?" Arlene set the stinky roses on the nearby credenza and pushed between Rosemary and Max. "First my roses and now the hedge? I've been training those bushes for years now." When she hurried out the door and across the yard, Rosemary, Max and Otis followed. "If you arrest this Peeping Tom person, I'm suing him for property damage, too." The older woman stopped in front of the gap of crushed branches in her leafy green hedge. Her shoulders sank with dismay. She picked up one of the broken stems, still full of green leaves and long thorns. "This is ruined. I'll have to plant a whole new shrub and trim the others down to match."

"I'll pay for the new bush, Arlene," Rosemary offered.

"Of course you will. This is your fault. And it's not as though you can't afford it."

For a split second, when Max reached around Arlene, Rosemary thought he was shoving her out of the way for being such a witch. Instead, he pulled loose a scrap of soggy black sweatshirt material that had caught on one of the bush's long thorns. He showed the tatter to Rosemary before holding it up for the Dinkles. "The man I chased wore a black hoodie. Have you ever seen anyone like that around here? The driver of that truck, perhaps?"

"Don't be ridiculous," Arlene answered first. "It's too hot to wear a sweatshirt, even at night. Ours are all packed up until the fall."

Max closed the torn material in his hand and stuffed it into the pocket of his jeans. "I didn't ask if you owned a black sweatshirt, Mrs. Dinkle. I asked if you'd seen anybody wearing one."

The dark-haired woman glanced up at her husband. But was that a plea for help out of talking herself into an awkward corner or the remembrance of something familiar in her eyes?

Otis, oblivious to any underlying message, threw up his hands. "Don't look at me. I have no idea where my old hoodie is."

"I don't suppose you could produce that hoodie, could you, Mr. Dinkle? Let me check to see if there's a chunk of cloth torn out of it?"

"You think my husband is spying on Rosemary, Detective? That he would threaten her?"

"Like I said, ma'am. I'm just here looking for some answers." Max wrapped his fingers around Rosemary's arm, indicating the interview was over. "If you two find that hoodie, or spot anyone else wearing one in the area, give me a call. Let me know if you see that truck again, too. Thank you for your help."

Rosemary hurried her steps to keep up with Max's long strides around the end of the hedge and across her yard to climb inside his blue Chevelle and head to their next appointment. As she buckled herself in, she waited for him to finish texting on his phone and asked, "We didn't find out anything useful from them, did we?"

"I'm asking Trent to see if he can run down the owner of that truck. It's a long shot, but it could be significant." He tucked the phone into his pocket before starting the car's powerful engine and backing out of the driveway. "We also found out that Otis was awake when our unsub was running through his yard. I can't believe that neighbors as curious as they are didn't go to the window when they heard me shouting. Unless one or both of them are hiding something. And we found out he owns a black hoodie—even if he claims to not know where it is."

"We've been friends and neighbors for years. Why would Otis want to kill me?"

"I don't know. Maybe he doesn't. But I can't imagine he's a very happily married man. I'm guessing he's got all sorts of hobbies to distract him from that shrew. Listening to music, running."

"You think scaring me to death qualifies as a hobby?"

Max reached across the center console to squeeze her hand. "The Dinkles' information might not mean a thing except that you need to find better neighbors. I'm figuring out all the pieces to the puzzle right now. Pretty soon we'll be able to discard the ones that don't fit, and put the right ones together and find our answers. We'll get this guy. Whoever it is. We'll clear your name.

I promise." He released her to shift the car into Drive. "Want to have a little fun?"

"I thought we were focusing on finding those puzzle pieces."

He grinned. "Not all day long. Hold on."

He gunned the souped-up engine and spit out a cloud of exhaust right in front of the Dinkles' house before speeding away.

Rosemary laughed when she saw, in the side-view mirror, Arlene's hand fly up and the woman launch into a tirade that had no place to go except at her poor husband. But Otis didn't put up with it for long. Arlene was probably still complaining about ruined hedges and smelly exhausts and who knew what else when Otis plugged in his earbuds, pulled his cap over his head and took off on his morning jog.

She turned and relaxed in the car's bucket seat. "You're naughty, Detective Krolikowski."

Max slid his mirrored sunglasses on. "Yep. I kind of am."

But her smile quickly faded when she considered the idea that turning her life upside down and forcing her to live like a recluse might be someone's idea of a hobby.

ROSIE STROLLED THE grand hallway on the executive floor of the Endicott Global building, studying the oil paintings and watercolors displayed on the paneled walls. Max stood close by, studying her.

The drive to the industrial park area north of downtown Kansas City had given Max the chance to get the Cold Case Squad up to speed on events from the past twenty-four hours. He'd dropped off the party-store recording device and the sick threat buried inside it at the precinct with Trent to see if the lab could get anything useful off the water-soaked items. Liv and her fiancé, Gabe Knight, who thought he recognized the society event in the photo with the young man Rosie had ID'd, were using his connections at the *Kansas City Journal* to track down a name. Trent had given the information about the dark green truck cruising Rosie's neighborhood to the team's information guru, Katie Rinaldi. If anyone could track down the owner of a truck with no license plate or VIN number, it was Katie and her magic computer tricks.

Right now, Max was playing a waiting game—his least favorite part of police work. Waiting for information from his team, waiting for the appointment that was running late...waiting for these feelings he had for Rosie to start making sense.

He'd been with a few women most of the world would consider prettier, and certainly more outgoing and daring than Rosie. But this was more than a pickup in a bar—a one-night stand before he moved on in the bright light of day. This was more than repaying a debt he owed an Army pilot he'd never met, more than an assignment Lieutenant Rafferty-Taylor had given him. Whatever was happening inside him, it was even more than doing for her what he hadn't been able to do for Jimmy. Whatever was going on between him and Rosie Posy was complicated and messy, unlike any sort of relationship he'd toyed with before.

Sure, her needy grabs and shy kisses could turn him inside out. A man could lose himself in her cool eyes and the warm scent of her hair. They'd talked. She'd listened. *He'd* listened. When the hell had that ever happened? He was no lothario, but her responses to his touch, whether it was a drunken kiss or a platonic cuddle, made him feel powerful, male—as if he might just be a decent catch for the right woman, after all. But how could a woman who was so wrong for a guy like him ever be the right one?

And since when did he get so philosophical about a woman or wanting to understand his feelings, anyway?

He had a job to do. Period. HUA. He wasn't going to let any distracting emotions cloud his judgment or get in the way of solving this murder again.

In a few long strides, Max caught up to Rosie. She seemed to like these paintings of farms and fruit and people he didn't know, hanging in gaudy gold and heavy wood frames that seemed more about showing off how much money Endicott Global made in a year rather than the art itself. Or maybe Rosie was just more capable of being patient and feigning interest than he'd ever be.

She'd stopped in front of a life-size oil painting of a white-haired man with a wizened face, standing in front of a fancy marble mantel. The old geezer's posture was surprisingly straight, which made Max think the guy was former military. But with his pin-striped suit, and thumb tucked into the watch pocket of his paisley vest, Max got the idea that the guy was more of a politician or businessman than anybody who'd gotten his hands dirty down in the trenches.

"He looks important," Rosie said, staring up at the painting.

Nope, he wasn't any good at pretending to be interested in something he wasn't. He went for prettier works of art himself. Like the woman draped over his randy body when he'd woken up this morning. He reached over and brushed a curling copper tendril off her cheek. She shivered when his fingertip circled around her ear. Yep, this lady was more responsive to his touch than she probably ought to be. "Why do you wear your hair like this? Don't tell me it's in deference to the summer heat."

She shrugged and moved a step beyond his reach. "It keeps my naturally wavy hair under control."

"You'd turn more heads if you lost a little bit of that control."

"I'm not interested in turning heads. I've been in the spotlight far more than I ever wanted to be. I already have bright red hair and pasty white skin." Warm copper silk and unblemished alabaster that was finer than the marble in that pretentious painting was a more accurate description in his mind. "It's calmer, easier to get through life, to be more subdued or conservative—whatever you want to call it—and not draw attention to myself."

"That's Bratcher's doing, not yours."

Rosie swiveled her gaze up to him. "That makes you angry?"

"Yeah. He's been dead six years. It pisses me off that that man can still hurt you."

"Wearing my hair in a bun hurts me?"

"Thinking you've got to have a certain look or act a certain way or else somebody's going to hurt you. Being afraid like that isn't right." He tugged at the tendril that had sprung back onto her cheek. "Be yourself. Tell the world what you want and go for it. I think there's some fire hiding under that ladylike facade of yours. Wear your hair down and loose if that's the way you like it, or shave it off in a buzz cut—which I hope like hell isn't what you really want."

"Max. Your language," she chided in a whisper, glancing over at the receptionist at the main desk. "We're in a public place."

Instead of apologizing, he fingered the top button of her blue-and-white dress. "Unhook a few of these. Good grief, woman, it's ninety-three degrees out there and it isn't even noon yet."

She swatted his hand away. "No."

His resentment of Richard Bratcher quickly gave way to a lopsided grin. "Told you there was fire in there."

And then he thought of the real reason she wore those high-necked dresses and his mood shifted again, raising her concern. "What is it?"

"Those scars are badges of honor. You survived. That takes real strength." Jimmy Stecher's worst wounds were far less visible. "I'd bet money you've got some form of PTSD, just like Jimmy did. I think of all the pain and guilt and fear Jimmy kept locked up inside him. Maybe if he hadn't believed he was all alone…if he'd known he could rail at me or talk or whatever he needed, I'd have been there for him. He shouldn't have tried to control every little thing. Clearly, he couldn't handle the pressure. No one can."

"Max. I'm not going to kill myself." Her soft voice pierced the heavy thoughts that had blurred his vision. She brushed her fingers against his, down at his thigh. "I've seen a therapist. I'm coping. Besides, I'm not alone. You're with me."

He turned his hand and captured hers in a solid grip. "Good. You're growing on me, Rosie. I'd hate to finally figure you out one day and then lose…"

Ah, hell. Max's thoughts all rolled together in a jumble. Lose what? Her? After just a few days, he wouldn't do anything so dumb as…anything that felt so right as… He'd fallen for Rosie March.

Max pulled his hand away and stuffed it into the back pocket of his jeans. Well, of course he had. When had he ever done anything the easy way? This was sure to come back and bite him in the butt. Because Rosie

March probably had no plans to ever fall in love again, and certainly not with a boorish, potty-mouthed tough guy like him.

Perhaps mistaking the source of his uncomfortable silence, Rosie changed the conversation to a more neutral topic. She pointed to the white-haired man in the painting. "Who do you think this is?"

The tapping of high heels on the marble flooring thankfully interrupted them. Dr. Hillary Wells walked up. "That is Dr. Lloyd Endicott. The founder of our company." Although Max recognized the older woman from the computer screen at the Cold Case Squad meeting, she was taller than he'd imagined. Her short, dark hair and high cheekbones were even more striking in person. She wore a pricey skirt and blouse beneath her stark white lab coat and, as Max remembered the preferential treatment from the meeting, he wasn't surprised that she extended her hand to Rosie first. "Hi. I'm Dr. Hillary Wells. You're here for an appointment?"

"Yes," Rosie answered.

He flashed his badge before shaking her hand. "Max Krolikowski, KCPD. This is my associate, Miss March."

Hillary gestured to the double doors behind the receptionist's desk, and they fell into step beside her. "Come into my office. I apologize for running late. Even though I'm overseeing the entire company now, I still like to keep my hand in the lab where I started—before Dr. Endicott discovered my talents and promoted me. Keeps a girl humble, you know. I was following up on some experiment results. If I'm recommending to the board that they up funding for a new product line, I want to make sure I know what I'm talking about."

After ordering coffee from her assistant and showing Rosie and Max to two guest chairs, she hung up her lab coat and pulled on a jacket that matched her skirt, instantly switching from scientist to CEO. She came back to her desk and opened a tub of hand cream. As she rubbed the cream into her skin, she pointed to the door, indicating the portrait of the distinguished gentleman Rosemary had asked about. "Lloyd started his research in a small lab not far from our location. Brilliant man. He developed a viable oral chemotherapy treatment with minimal side effects. A dozen patents later, he had multiple labs doing the research for him, he was building production facilities around the world, and Endicott Global went public." She sat in her chair behind the desk, her tone growing wistful. "The man died a billionaire, but he was always happiest puttering around in the lab."

"He sounds like a father figure to you," Rosie suggested.

"Very much so," Hillary agreed. "He was certainly a mentor of mine. We worked closely together for a number of years. I suppose that's why he handpicked me to succeed him. He had no children of his own and had been a widower for some time."

"I was close to my father, too. You must miss him."

"I do. Lloyd was an elderly man, but he was always young at heart." Her assistant brought them each a coffee and slipped out as quietly as he'd come in. Dr. Wells took a few moments to drink a sip and compose herself. "He was taken from us far too soon. Terrible car accident."

Rosie cradled her mug in her lap, probably feeling real empathy for the other woman, or maybe just thinking about how much she missed her own dad. "I'm so sorry."

"Thank you." Hillary swallowed another sip, then set her mug aside. She grew more businesslike and turned her attention to Max. "Now. How may I help you, Detective? You're following up on the report KCPD sent me?"

"Yes, ma'am." Hopefully, he'd be able to uncover a more useful puzzle piece here. "The Richard Bratcher case? The ME found a toxic amount of RUD-317, a drug your company produces, in his system. Can you tell us about it?"

Dr. Wells picked up a pair of reading glasses and opened a folder on her desk to skim the file. "Ah, yes. After reading your ME's report, I asked my assistant to pull the pharmaceutical file. So what are your questions about the drug?"

Rosie moved to the edge of her seat and set her coffee mug on the desk. "You keep calling it a drug. But it poisoned Richard. Surely, it's not still on the market."

"RUD-317 is used for the treatment of certain cancers. It targets and reduces malignant tumor growth. In some applications it eradicates the cancerous growth completely. In others, it contains the malignancy." Dr. Wells thumbed through her file and pulled out a thick set of papers stapled together. "Six years ago it was brand-new on the market. These are the drug trials immediately preceding that time to tell us who had access to RUD-317 outside of the lab. Our staff, of course, is all bonded, with signed confidentiality agreements. It would be impossible for one of them to get the drug out of the lab. Every shift goes through a security check when they leave."

Max bit down on the urge to argue her point. Nothing was impossible if you knew the right person and had the right leverage.

"Richard was never sick a day in his life. If he had cancer, he never told me." Was that distress he heard in Rosie's voice? Did she really care that that monster might have been battling cancer?

"You knew Mr. Bratcher personally?"

"Yes."

"Not every patient chooses to share with his loved ones when he has a serious illness."

Rosie sank back in her chair, her confusion and unease with this conversation making her press her pretty mouth into a grim line and her eye focus drop to that self-conscious, don't-notice-me level she used as a defense mechanism.

Max reached across the space between their chairs to squeeze her hand. When that gray gaze darted over to meet his, he winked, silently encouraging her not to give up the fight. Then he released her and turned his attention back to Dr. Wells. "If you read the ME's report again, Doctor, you'll see he wasn't being treated with the drug. Bratcher wasn't sick." Not physically sick, at any rate. "Either he had access to the drug himself, or someone on your list there had a motive for killing him."

The dark-haired CEO sat up ramrod straight, clearly displeased with him questioning her authority. She held up the packet of paper. "All I can tell you is that there is a Bratcher in this study. He could have been part of the placebo group, or he could have been a legitimate patient who was cured and continued to use the drug against our advisement."

Dr. Wells set the packet down, rested her elbows on top of it and steepled her fingers. Here it came. The lecture telling Max that he, the Cold Case Squad and ME's office had to be wrong. Because Dr. High-and-Mighty there was always right.

"Our report, in conjunction with the ME's autopsy, indicates that your Mr. Bratcher had consumed a far bigger dose than recommended, or multiple doses over a short period of time. There was a huge quantity of RUD-317 in his system. More than enough to trigger the convulsions, aspiration of stomach contents and suffocation that led to his death." She sat back in her chair, blithely unaware or uncaring of how the gruesome details surrounding Bratcher's death made Rosie go pale. "If Mr. Bratcher was murdered, then you have to prove how all that medication got into his system. Someone could have opened the capsules and slipped the RUD-317 into his food or drink, or replaced some other medication he regularly took without his knowledge. But unless you can prove any of that, all you have is a drug overdose, and Endicott Global is not responsible."

Max pushed to his feet. This interview was done. Dr. Wells had gone CEO on them, more interested in protecting her company and its profits from a potential lawsuit than in helping them solve a murder.

Max thanked her for the coffee and little else. "I'll need a list of all the patients in that clinical trial, and any staff, researchers or salespeople who would have had access to the drug six years ago. Maybe one of them had a grudge against Bratcher. It could be a disgruntled client, or somebody he took for a lot of money."

Dr. Wells closed the file and stood, also. "I'll have my assistant forward the staff contacts later today. Patient names are confidential, however. You'll need a warrant for me to share that."

"My lieutenant's already working on it."

"Then as soon as my office receives it, I'll get you a list of everyone who had contact with the drug."

Max was ready to leave, but Rosie was a class act all the way. "Thank you for your time, Dr. Wells."

"Glad to help." The CEO followed Max and Rosie to the door. "Detective Krolikowski, I can't believe that anyone employed by Endicott Global or its affiliates would abuse our drugs and knowingly hurt someone.

We take too much pride in our work, in our mission to save lives."

"Nonetheless, I want that list."

"Very well." She caught the door before Max could close it behind them and extended her hand to Rosie again. "Rosemary? Perhaps I'll see you at one of the museum's upcoming fund-raisers. I sit on the city's cultural arts board. We're always looking for new donors to support the arts in Kansas City."

Rosie shook the doctor's hand and nodded her thanks to the invitation. But when he would have expected her to quickly pull away, Rosie continued to hold on for an awkward length of time. What was that redhead up to?

"Dr. Wells, did you have access to RUD-317 six years ago?"

The two women locked gazes. To her brave credit, Rosie wasn't the first one to look away. Hillary ended the handshake and gave the door a nudge, herding them out. "Of course I did. I helped Lloyd create it. But I never even met your Mr. Bratcher. Why on earth would I want to kill him?"

The door snapped firmly shut in their faces. Suddenly, Dr. Wells's assistant was there to walk them to the elevator. Max glanced down at Rosie. "I guess our meeting's over."

Once the elevator doors closed behind them and they were alone, Max sat back against the railing and asked, "What was that handshake thing about?"

"I can't be certain. Maybe it's a woman's intuition, or perhaps an old memory is trying to surface."

"I need a little more to follow what you're getting at."

She thrust her right hand at his face. "Smell that."

"Whoa." Max grinned and ducked to one side to avoid an accidental punch to the chin. But he caught a whiff of what Rosie was talking about. He laced his fingers together with hers and drew her hand to his nose again. He breathed in the floral scent of Hillary Wells's hand cream. "You said you smelled perfume on the sheets in Bratcher's hotel room that day."

Rosie nodded. "I just assumed it was Charleen Grimes who'd spent the night with Richard. But maybe there was someone else there, a different woman." She pulled her hand away and wrapped it around the strap of her purse. She leaned against the back wall beside him. "Six years is a long time to try to pinpoint an exact scent, and it's probably not anything that could help you make an arrest—"

"But it's another potential piece of the puzzle."

Chapter Ten

Rosemary followed Max off the elevator onto the top floor that housed the office suites of Howard's law firm. The day had been a long one. She was hungry for dinner. She'd love a long swim to ease the tension from her muscles. Duchess and Trixie were probably dancing around the house to be let out to do their business. She was done talking to people who wouldn't give her straight answers.

And ever since the idea of Otis Dinkle spying on her had been put into her head, she'd felt as though someone had been following her all day as Max carted her from interview to interview—keeping her in sight, keeping her safe. Max assured her they were gathering useful clues, expanding KCPD's list of suspects and crossing others off the list who either had an alibi or lacked a motive to kill Richard and threaten her.

More than anything, she wanted to go home to her quiet little house and be surrounded by her parents' things and her beloved pets. Maybe she and Max would get to talk. Maybe he'd see the chance to steal another kiss and take it. And maybe, if her scars and the self-confidence that sometimes failed her hadn't been too much of a turnoff, he'd offer another night in his sheltering arms and she'd know a second night of blissful sleep. He'd said she had to be bold and ask for what she wanted—that he was no good at reading between the lines and guessing. Well, what she wanted was to go home. With him.

But when she opened her mouth to say as much, Charleen Grimes unfolded her long legs from the couch in the center of the room and crossed the floor in her three-inch heels.

"That's Charleen Grimes," she whispered, instead.

"The mistress?" Max clarified. Rosemary would have turned around, gone back downstairs and walked home if Max's hand hadn't been at her back, drawing her forward beside him. He dipped his face beside her ear and whispered, "The woman needs some meat on her bones. Your ex must have had a thing for making love to sticks." He turned his fingers to pat the swell of Rosie's hip. "I'll take a real woman any day."

"Bless you, Max." Rosie's chin lifted a little higher at the praise. "Good evening, Charleen."

"Well, if it isn't the little murderess herself."

Howard stepped out of his office at the end of the hallway and hurried to join them. "Charleen, you are way out of line." He snapped his fingers to the receptionist for her to notify Mr. Austin that his client had arrived for her KCPD interview. "Remember our conversation about slandering my client."

"*I'm* out of line?" She ran her painted nails along the lapel of her blue silk jacket. "Which one of us is here to be questioned as a murder suspect?" Charleen's blue eyes narrowed. "You and your nine million dollars took Richard from me. I will never forgive you."

A sad realization washed over Rosemary. "You really loved him, didn't you?"

"A lot more than you ever did."

Most certainly. "Did you love him so much that you'd rather see him dead than with anybody else?"

"How dare you, you little mouse. I'm the only one who wants justice for Richard. All you're concerned about is saving your own skin."

"Justice?" Rosie's blood turned to ice in her veins. How many of those crude threats had mentioned justice for Richard? Were Charleen's words a horrid coincidence? A slip of the tongue? Or was there something much more ominous and far too familiar in the accusation?

Charleen took another step and Max's hand shot between them to keep the woman from coming any closer. "Stay with me, Rosie." His blue eyes met hers with a pinpoint focus, probably checking to make sure she didn't slip into another one of those trancelike states where she was paralyzed with fear. She blinked, nodded, silently reassured him she wasn't so upset by the other woman's words that she couldn't function. "Maybe I'd better handle this interview on my own," he suggested.

Howard was instantly at Rosemary's side. "Perhaps so, Detective. I don't know why you have her out doing your job."

Max's shoulders came back at the irritation in Howard's voice. Thankfully, he didn't take the bait and continue the argument. "Just get her someplace safe for twenty or thirty minutes, okay?"

"My pleasure." Howard's cool hand cupped her elbow, pulling her away from Max. "You're welcome to wait in my office while your friend conducts his business."

"Thanks." While Howard tucked Rosemary's hand into the crook of his elbow and led her to his back corner office, Max escorted Charleen in the opposite direction to Mr. Austin's suite at the end of the hallway.

"What's that perfume you're wearing?" he asked. "It's sexy as all get-out."

"Don't try to charm me, Detective Krolikowski. You haven't got the chops for it."

The man wasn't as clueless as he pretended to be. "So I can't buy that scent for my girlfriend?"

Charleen stopped and leveled a glare at Rosemary. "No."

Girlfriend? Was that part of his investigative bag of tricks to get a suspect talking—using her as the proverbial burr that could get Charleen agitated underneath her saddle? Or could there be a grain of truth in that one word? Rosemary's pulse did a funny little pitter-patter at the hope that he might be halfway serious about claiming her as his.

But Charleen's hateful gaze was a painful reminder that Rosemary needed this part of her life to be over. Charleen pouted her ruby-red lips into a smile and linked her arm through Max's, figuratively taking from Rosemary what Charleen claimed Rosemary had taken from her. The tall blonde sashayed her hip into Max's as their voices faded down the long hallway, and Rosie's nostrils flared with an emotion that was far closer to feeling possessive about Max than feeling inadequate lined up next to a woman whose beauty she couldn't match. "It's a personal scent, designed especially for me. Back in my modeling days—"

"Don't let her get to you. Charleen's a bitter, vindictive woman." Howard closed the outer office door and followed Rosemary into his private office, locking the door behind him. Was he that worried about the tall blonde causing a scene that would upset her? "In her own way, I think she truly loved Richard. But she didn't handle all the other women and one-night stands as well as you did."

Rosemary's laugh held little humor. "I don't think I handled his cheating well at all." She dropped her purse into one of the guest chairs and sat in the other, leaning back and closing her weary eyes. "It does devastating things to a woman's ego and ability to trust when she finds out she's not enough for her man."

"Are you enough for Krolikowski?"

Her eyes fluttered open at the unexpected question. "Excuse me?"

Howard shrugged and crossed to the wet bar in the corner. "I couldn't help but notice how chummy the two of you have gotten these past few days."

She sat up straighter. "We're working together. I finally have someone at KCPD treating me like the victim, not a prime suspect."

"Seemed friendlier than that to me." He held up a mug. "Coffee?"

"Please."

Friendlier? Certainly Max had become important to her these past few days. He'd been the only one to believe that the threats against her were real and not some scam to gain sympathy or divert attention onto another suspect in KCPD's Cold Case Squad investigation. Okay, so it had taken a little blackmail in the form of appealing to his military roots to finally get him to listen. But once he saw the damage to her front porch and read the notes, he believed. He protected. He upset her small, familiar world in frightening, exciting ways, and yet he made her feel safe. So, yes, they'd become friends—an opposites attracting, differences complementing each other kind of thing. But something in her heart wanted them to be much more.

Once this case was solved, however—assuming they could piece all the old secrets together to complete the puzzle and finally solve Richard's murder—would she be enough to interest a man like Max? Would there be other reasons he might want to remain a part of her life?

"Here you go." Howard handed her a mug of the steaming brew and took a seat on the corner of his desk, facing her. He swallowed a drink, then splayed his fingers and looked at his hand before rubbing his knuckles against the leg of his lightweight wool slacks. "Is he making any progress? Getting the job done?"

Rosemary cradled the warm mug between her hands. "You know how important it is to me to clear my name. It's the only way to convince Charleen and my neighbors and the rest of the world that I didn't get away with murder. Maybe I could get a job teaching again. Max is helping change people's opinion of me. He's expanded the list of suspects so that my name's not the only one on it for a change. He makes it more comfortable for me to interact with people." She shook her head. "I still can't claim that it's easy—my trust issues make it hard to socialize for long with big groups or certain people, of course—but he makes it easier to try."

"Good for him." Howard set his mug on the desk and scratched at a trio of welts on his left hand. "I made life easier for you, too, if you remember. I kept you from ever being formally charged for Richard's murder by reminding the police they didn't have enough evidence to take the case to the DA for prosecution."

"I appreciate that, Howard. I don't know how I would have gotten through the last six years without you. You were so helpful with Stephen's case, too." When she saw how badly the red marks were irritating him, she set her mug on the desk, too, and got up to cradle his big hand between hers. "Where did you get those nasty scratches? I think you need some hydrocortisone or calamine..."

Puncture wounds. A dermatitis reaction to a foreign substance, like leaf sap or pollen.

Rosemary released his hand and backed away as if his skin had burned her. He'd grappled with a hawthorn bush. "You?"

The dark eyes looking back at her were anything but friendly, patient or professional. That hard, cold, disappointed look was a lot like...his brother's.

"The canned laughter was a little theatrical, but that scream of yours was worth every penny."

Rosie glanced at the door. Did she need to run? Would he really hurt her? "I thought you were my friend."

Howard's voice was laced with contempt. "And I thought you were smart."

Rosie dropped her chin and shivered. So talking was out. Ingrained habits from an abusive relationship were hard to break. She felt herself tensing, bracing, preparing herself for whatever cruel words would spew from his mouth. She inched away as the dimensions of the locked room closed in on her.

He'd trapped her.

Just like his brother had.

Only, she wasn't alone in her house with a dangerously unpredictable man. She wasn't alone at all. Max was right down the hallway. Okay, about a hundred feet down that hallway. With at least three closed doors in between them.

Rosie's chin shot up as she shook off the crippling fears of the past. She grabbed her purse and dashed to the door.

But Howard beat her to it. Moving surprisingly fast for an older man, he planted himself between her and escape. She quickly circled behind his desk and leather chair, scanning the room for an available weapon if she needed to defend herself.

"I lost my brother because of you," Howard accused.

"I didn't kill him."

"I don't care who did. I'm just glad he's gone." He moved to the desk and Rosie backed up to the window. "He was blowing through the family fortune, ruining the firm with his indiscretions. That's why he latched on to you—for the money and respectability."

"You're not like him, Howard. Please. You were kind to Stephen. You took care of our legal and financial needs. You helped me get Richard out of my life."

"Damn right, I did. You owe me. I've been there for you every step of the way. I was patient with you and all your little idiosyncrasies." As he came around the desk, she countered his path, keeping as much distance as possible between them. The wary beat of her pulse nearly choked her. If he laid a hand on her the way Richard had… "You depend on me," he reminded her. "When you started getting those threats, when your mysterious stalker knew so many intimate details about you and Richard and said he wanted to kill you, I knew you were afraid."

"I was terrified. Why would you do that to me?"

He pounded his fist on the desk and she jumped. "So you would come to me for help. Not to some uncivilized thug of a cop. Good grief, I heard you picked him up in a bar. You're my class of people, Rosemary, not his."

"That uncivilized thug is right down the hall, Howard. I'll scream and he'll throw you in jail so fast—"

"He can't hear you through soundproofed walls. And I have a feeling Charleen won't be a very cooperative witness and that her interview will take a while. Long enough for you to come to your senses and remember who your real hero is."

Her gaze darted from the thick walls lined with books to the tenth-story window and locked door that offered her only means of escape. "I'm not that frightened mental invalid beaten down by grief and abuse anymore. The real me is coming back. Max!"

When she charged toward the door, Howard shifted direction and snatched her arm, pulling her against him and slapping his other hand over her mouth to silence her. "You won't scream, because I'll have his badge if you do."

Rosie froze in his painful grip and he moved his sweaty palm off her lips. "You'd do that? You'd ruin his career?"

Howard laughed. "It'd be easy enough. Krolikowski is already on thin ice with the department. Public drunkenness. Anger issues—"

"He's not like that—"

"—a blatant disregard for regulations and comportment. He'd probably come in here and beat me up if he could hear you. Imagine the mileage I'd get out of that with the commissioner."

She tugged against the hand on her arm. "I'd tell his superior officers the truth. You're crazy."

"Oh, *I'm* crazy? Says the thirty-something recluse who lives inside a fortress, dresses like an old maid and is afraid of her own shadow? You think they'd take the word of a murder suspect over a respected member of the court?" His moist breath spit against her ear. "Whatever you think you have with him is done. *I'm* the man you need. You're going to marry me."

Her hips butted against his desk. His thighs trapped her. "Never. You threatened to kill me, Howard."

"I would have married you and made the threats all go away. That was the plan. I wanted you so scared that you'd have to come out of that cave you hide in and turn to someone for help. And it was working until Krolikowski came along." He flattened his hand against his chest. "It was supposed to be me. For six years I've planned how we would be together. I showed you more patience than any normal man could. I set it up so that *I* was the man in your life."

"You were my friend."

"People have married for less."

"I don't love you."

"That doesn't matter. We could have a successful business partnership. I'm more mature than my brother ever was. I wouldn't make demands on you."

She lowered her chin and shook her head. "That damn money."

"Now that's hardly ladylike. Krolikowski's bad habits are rubbing off on you." He spoke to her cowed head. "I've earned you, you freak. I sided with you against my brother's memory. I was loyal to you. I did everything I could for your loser brother. Who else would have you?"

"If that's the deal you're offering, I'd rather be alone." When she zeroed in on his Italian loafers, she felt a flare of red-haired temper flooding through her. She was done being the Bratcher brothers' victim.

She brought her heel down hard on his instep and shoved her shoulder into his chest, freeing herself. Howard stumbled back into a bookshelf and she ran for the door. "Max!"

All she had to do was scream if she was in trouble, and he'd come running. No matter how many floors or doors were between them. He'd promised.

"Max!" Ignoring Howard's threat, she threw open the door.

"Your choice. His career is over. You will not leave me for him."

"I was never yours."

He cinched his hands around her waist and tossed her toward the desk. She bruised her hip against the corner, but he was there before she could scramble away, capturing her against the solid oak. "He's rough, exciting, animalistic, I bet."

"What is wrong with you?" Rosie clawed at his neck, beat at his chest. "Get your hands off me. He's going to arrest you."

Howard bent her back over the desk, his thigh sliding between hers. She slapped at the hand that skimmed her breast. "Is that how you like it? Rough? I don't have to be a gentleman. All these years I thought that was what you wanted. But I could send you a few more love notes if you want."

"Get. Off. Me." Her shoulder hit a coffee mug, sloshing the hot liquid onto her arm. Forget the Colonel's empty Army pistol. She reached up, closed her hand around the mug and tossed the hot liquid in his face. She wasn't the only one screaming when she ran for the door. "Max!"

But she'd only riled the beast. Before she made it to the door, Howard caught her and shoved her up against the bookshelf. He closed his hands around her neck in a choke hold that cut off her voice and her breath and stuck his red, scalded face near hers. "I always wondered what it was like when Richard got rough with you."

Rosie twisted, gouged, kicked. She tried to suck in a breath, but the sound gurgled in her throat. Her chest constricted. Ached. Howard had lost it. There was no reasoning with him now.

"Rosie!" A fist pounded on the locked door.

Maybe Howard hadn't heard the same angry shout she had. He tightened his grip around her neck. "There *is* a little rush to this, isn't there? I can feel the pulse points beneath my thumbs. Does it hurt? Do you feel like doing what I ask now?"

Pound. Pound. "Rosie!"

She scratched at his injured hand, but she was getting weak. She needed air. White dots floated across her vision and the room tilted.

"If you don't say yes to me, I'll make sure you go away for Richard's murder. I know enough details about your relationship to make you look guilty as sin. I'll even defend you…and, sadly, lose your case." He nuzzled her ear. "What will it be? Boyfriend or me? Prison? Or marri—"

The frame around the door splintered and the heavy oak swung open beside her. Max rammed Howard like a linebacker, tearing his grip off Rosie, freeing her. The two men flew across the desk and Rosie collapsed to her knees. She sucked in a deep breath that scratched her throat and filled her deprived lungs with precious oxygen. A chair toppled, another broke.

"Max." Her voice came out in a hoarse croak. His fist met Howard's jaw with a thud, and the attorney's head snapped back. "Max!"

"You keep your hands off her. Understand?"

Howard laughed in response, not putting up any fight. "Temper, temper, Officer. Oh, I am so reporting this. Cop Attacks Attorney."

"The attorney's a nut job." Max flipped Howard face-down on the carpet, put his knee in the man's back and cuffed him.

His grizzled jaw was tight when he reached over to touch Rosie's bruised neck and arm. "He hurt you."

"I'm okay. I'll be okay." Her voice was getting stronger. The room blossomed with color again after she'd nearly passed out. Max's blue eyes. The red blood at the corner of Howard's mouth. Rosie pushed to her feet, leaning on the shelves for support. "Howard sent those threats. It makes sense. He knew the details of my relationship with his brother. He wanted to scare me so I'd turn to him. Fall for him, maybe." Howard giggled like a child as Max helped him into a chair. She averted her gaze from those crazy cold eyes and looked to the man who had saved her. Again. "I turned to you, instead."

"You're sure you're okay?" He palmed the back of her neck and pulled her onto her toes for a quick, hard kiss that left her a little breathless again. His chest expanded in quick, deep inhales after the brief fight and sprint down the hallway. "Thank God you can scream, woman. I don't want to think about what could have happened if I'd been even a few seconds late. I had the receptionist call 9-1-1. Uniformed officers should be here any minute."

In the meantime, Rosie didn't complain when he hooked his arm around her shoulders and pulled her against him. She was quickly learning that this was where she felt the safest. "He was no better than Richard. How do I keep attracting these winners?" she added, the sarcasm clear, even in her husky tone.

Max went quiet for a few seconds, then covered the silence with a wry little laugh. "I'll throw his butt in jail for a very long time."

But Rosie tugged on his shirt, stopping him midreport. "Howard didn't kill Richard. He's hardly a perfume kind of guy. And how would he get his hands on RUD-317?"

"He could be the Bratcher in that pharmaceutical trial Dr. Wells is holding on to." He tapped the shoulder of the curiously subdued man sitting on his cuffed hands. "Hey. How about it, Bratcher?"

Howard grew more subdued as the manic thrill he'd discovered when he'd been choking her subsided. She could tell he was thinking more like a lawyer than the man with the violent obsession who'd brought a baseball bat and terror to her home. "I don't know what you're talking about."

"Can I at least book him for making terroristic threats to you?"

"Be my guest." Rosie nodded, wishing she felt more relief at finally identifying the man who'd preyed on her darkest fears.

Max didn't seem to think this was over yet, either. "We've got two perps—Howie here and the woman who killed his brother six years ago. Ah, hell." Max pulled her toward the broken door to look out into the lobby but stopped when he realized he'd be leaving Howard unguarded if he went any farther. "Charleen Grimes just left with her attorney." He pulled out his cell and punched in a number. "I'm calling the team. We're gonna end this thing."

MAX LEANED AGAINST the Chevelle's front fender while Rosie finished giving her statement to Olivia Watson. He nodded to Jim Parker, walking past with a large evidence bag holding the black sweatshirt hoodie with the torn sleeve he'd found in the trunk of Howard Bratcher's car.

A car. Why couldn't the attorney drive a fancy green

pickup truck like the one Arlene Dinkle had reported seeing in the neighborhood? Now that would make the puzzle come together all neat and pretty. But Bratcher didn't own a truck. Maybe it was nothing but coincidence that an unidentified vehicle would show up in the same time frame as each of Bratcher's visits to Rosie's house. But, like most of the cops he knew, Max didn't like coincidences. If a good cop looked hard enough, there was almost always a rational explanation out there somewhere. Did the green truck mean someone else was watching Rosie's house? Their killer, perhaps? Or had Arlene made the whole thing up?

The truck wasn't the only piece to the puzzle that was bothering him. The summer night was still plenty warm, but Rosie kept running her hands up and down her bare arms as she and Liv talked over by Liv's SUV, as though she had a chill she just couldn't shake. Max wanted to put his hands there and warm her up. No, what he really wanted was to get her out of here—away from the flashing lights and endless questions and Howard Bratcher locked in the back of Trent's SUV to someplace quiet where they could be alone. Where he could hold her long enough to chase away that chill.

"Did you send a unit to keep an eye on Charleen Grimes?"

Max pulled away from the car at the approach of his lieutenant, Ginny Rafferty-Taylor, straightening to a civilian version of attention as his team leader came up beside him. "Yes, ma'am. If she goes anywhere besides home or her shop, or does anything suspicious, we'll know about it."

"In the meantime, we got a copy of that list of drug test patients and research and production staff from Endicott Global. Katie's going over it with a fine-tooth comb to see if Charleen's name pops—or any other family or business associate who could have gotten her access to the drug." The lieutenant tucked her short, silvery-blond hair behind her ears and leaned her hips back against the car the way he had a moment earlier. "You did good work today, Max."

He slid his fingers into the back pockets of his jeans and shrugged his frustration. "I haven't solved our case yet."

"Take the compliment. We've been working this murder for six years now. This is the first forward progress we've made in almost that long." She nodded toward the conversation wrapping up near the building's front door. "Miss March filled me in on the threats Howard Bratcher made against your badge, too. Don't worry. I've got your back. I didn't settle for just anybody on my squad. You were all handpicked for your various expertise."

"I gave Bratcher a fat lip." He eyed the purple bruises already appearing on Rosie's pale skin as she paused beneath a streetlight before crossing the street to join them. He felt his fingers curling into fists again. Was that supposed to be his area of expertise? Laying a guy out flat for nearly squeezing the life out of a woman? "I suppose I have an anger management class in my future?"

"You were protecting someone you care about." The lieutenant leaned in and whispered, "Besides, didn't I ever tell you I have a soft spot for big guys who are good with their hands?"

"No."

She squeezed his arm before walking away to her car. "You should meet my husband sometime."

Max chuckled. "Yes, ma'am."

Rosie exchanged good-nights with the lieutenant before joining Max at the car.

"Cold?" Max brushed his hands over the goose bumps dotting her arms.

She shook her head and shivered anew. "Confused, maybe. Disappointed in my inability to function out in the real world."

"That's harsh."

"Tonight made me feel like I'm not meant to be anything more than a prize to be stolen or swindled. Howard was so angry. Just like Richard." She raised her gaze to his. "Why couldn't I see it? Why did I think Howard was my friend?"

"Because you've got a heart, Rosie March." He opened the car door and pulled his black leather jacket from the backseat to drape around her shoulders. "Here. I think it's human nature to trust people, to want to see the best in them. Especially if that's the way they want you to see them. Most people keep their deepest thoughts and insecurities and shortcomings hidden. Good people and bad." He freed a couple of tendrils from the collar of the jacket. "I'm glad the bad things in this world haven't warped you like me yet."

She linked her fingers with his and held on when he would have pulled away. "I'm always going to believe you're a good guy, Max. Thank you. I can never repay you for listening to me, believing me. Jimmy would have been proud of you for standing by me and helping me get Howard out of my life."

"Just promise me if you meet anyone else named Bratcher, you'll run the other way instead of making friends."

At last, she smiled. "I promise." She braced her free hand against his chest and stretched up to kiss his cheek. "You did great, Sergeant. Thank you."

"Why does that sound like goodbye?" He tugged on

her fingers and led her around to the passenger seat. "I live in your basement."

"But I thought—with Howard under arrest…"

This mission wasn't over yet, as far as he was concerned. "There's still a killer out there I'm looking for. And we've stirred up enough of a hornet's nest today that I'm not letting you out of my sight until we identify the woman who was in Bratcher's bedroom that night and I can close my case." He opened the car door for her to get in. "Buckle up."

Her smile eased his concern a fraction. "Yes, sir."

By the time he'd circled back to the driver's side, Trent was jogging up to meet him. "Hey, brother."

"What is it, junior?"

His partner handed him a DMV printout of Glasses Guy, the man Rosie had ID'd from the society page photo. "Meet Leland Asher's nephew, Matthew."

"Son of a gun." He handed the printout over to Rosie. "Look familiar?"

"That's him. Is he part of his uncle's organization?" She handed the paper back. "What's his connection to me?"

"It may not mean anything. We can't tie him to any criminal wrongdoing," Trent answered. "But he does visit his uncle in prison."

"So he could be a courier for getting his uncle's messages in or out of Jeff City." Max quickly skimmed the rest of the information on the page and muttered a curse. Matt Asher drove a Chrysler sedan, not a green pickup. "So he doesn't have a connection to the Bratchers, either."

Trent shook his head. "He's got an alibi for most of the nights the stalker was at Rosie's house."

"Which is?"

"Believe it or not—therapy. He sees a clinical psychologist. I'm guessin' he's got family issues. We'll keep an eye on him to see if any messages are passed between him and Uncle Leland when he visits him in prison. But right now, we've got nothing on him. We can't touch him. Plus, the kid's only twenty-two. He was barely old enough to drive when Bratcher was murdered."

Max looked up to his partner and thanked him.

"Not a problem. Anything else?"

"Yeah. Send somebody over to watch Rosie's house tonight. I need some solid shut-eye."

Trent waved to Rosie to reassure her, as well. "I'll be there myself as soon as I process Bratcher."

"I owe ya."

"Don't worry, brother. I'll collect."

Max and the dogs heard the quiet whimpering over the rainfall sounds of the shower coming through the bathroom door. He didn't know about Duchess and Trixie, but he wasn't sure how long he could stand that heartbreaking little mewl before he busted down another door to get inside and do something about it.

The house couldn't be locked up any tighter. He had his Glock strapped to his belt. The blinds throughout the house were drawn to dissuade the Dinkles' and anyone else's curiosity about the copper-haired recluse, and he knew Trent was parked in his truck out in the driveway tonight. So no way had anyone gotten past all those lines of defense to hurt her.

Still… He knocked softly at the door. "Rosie? Honey, are you okay?"

"Just a minute." Although he could easily jimmy the old door lock, he scrubbed his hand over his stubbled jaw, waiting impatiently through some sniffling and shuffling noises. Then the running water stopped.

A few seconds later, the latch turned and the door opened.

"You girls, stay," he ordered. Not waiting for an invitation, he slipped inside the white-and-black-tiled bathroom and closed the door behind him.

"What is it?" Rosie asked, clutching the lime-green towel that hung from the scalloped swells of her breasts down to the top of her thighs. His pulse rate kicked up in hungry awareness, so he wisely hung back by the door. "Is something wrong?"

"I hope not." Ignoring the long, wavy strands of wet copper that clung to her shoulders and sent tiny rivulets of water down her arms and into the shadowy cleft between her breasts, Max focused on the ugly marks marring the skin around her neck. He brushed his fingers across the blue-and-violet bruises there. "Are you in pain? Is your throat still sore? The paramedic said that gargling would help." He ran through the checklist of possible complications related to her assault. "Are you having any trouble breathing or swallowing? Maybe I should have run you to the ER instead of bringing you home."

She offered him an unconvincing smile. "I'm okay. I'm sore. But the hot water helps."

So, no physical pain. That would have been easier to deal with. With the pad of his thumb, he wiped away a tear that lingered on her cheek. "And this?"

She turned her head and pressed a kiss into his palm. "You once said that I could tell you anything, that you'd listen."

"That's right." He made a valiant effort to avert his gaze from all that creamy bare skin peeking out above and below the edges of the towel. But the burn scars and bruises at her neck were a sobering reminder to his traitorous body that she wanted to have a serious conversation here. "Is everything okay?"

"You said I should look you in the eye and ask for what I want." She tilted those soft gray eyes to his and he lost his heart to her a little more. "I want you to stay."

"I wasn't planning on going back to the basement."

"No. I'm not saying this right." Her gaze dropped to his chin, then bounced right back. "Stay here. With me."

The walls of restraint that were keeping his libido in check took a serious hit. But he didn't want to misunderstand. "Honey, don't tease a man. Are you asking me to take you to bed?"

She nodded and reached up to trace her fingers along the line of his jaw, waking dozens of very interested nerve endings there. "I want to do more than cuddle tonight, Sergeant. I want to feel like a normal, desirable woman. I want to feel good hands, safe hands…*your* hands on me. I want to erase—"

"I get the message." Max already had her in his arms. His mouth was on hers, his tongue driving inside to claim her taste for his own. He drove her back against the tile wall, imprinting her curves against his harder body. Her hands slid up to his face and hair and his slid down to grasp her hips and pull them into the cradle of his thighs.

His jeans felt thick. His shirt was an impediment. And that towel definitely had to go.

With their lips clinging to each other, their hands explored places that were tender and hard. Silky and soft. Cool and hot. He got his belt off and his holster safely set aside on the vanity before she reached for the zipper of his jeans.

"Not yet, honey." He caught her wrists and moved her hands to his chest, encouraging her to go after the buttons on his shirt while he shucked out of his boots and jeans.

By the time he was as naked as she was and he'd fished a condom out of his wallet, her lips had discovered the taut, eager nipples of his chest and a bundle of nerves behind his left ear. He'd feasted on her lips and filled his hands with the heavy weight of her breasts. He tongued his way from one curve to the next, stopping only to turn the shower back on and adjust the temperature to a soothing warmth before he palmed the back of her thighs and lifted her into the shower with him.

"Max," she gasped, her thighs clenching when the water first hit her skin.

"Easy, honey." He pulled her into the heat of his body and switched positions, taking the brunt of the spray on his back. "I want to make this as good for you as I can."

Then he grabbed the bar of soap and really went to work. She wanted to forget that Howard had touched her? That Richard had abused her? Max wanted to imprint himself all over her body. He put his hands every place he could touch—her feet, her legs, that sweet round bottom. He washed her stomach and back and arms and breasts, running the creamy soap over her beautiful skin. Then he moved the soap between her legs to wash her there.

Her thighs clenched around his hand. Her fingers dug into his shoulders. Her forehead fell against his chest. "Oh, Max. Max." She said his name, over and over, in breathless whispers against his skin. Soon, he set the soap aside. With the heat of the water and the heat of his hand pressing against her most tender flesh, he felt her tighten, quiver. And when he slipped a finger inside her, then two, she cried out his name and convulsed around his hand.

How could any man not think this brave, vibrant, responsive woman was anything but sexy and desirable?

But it wasn't enough. For either of them.

The shy siren with the beautiful body slipped her arms around his neck and pressed every decadent inch against his hot, primed body. Not even the water sluicing over his head and shoulders could come between them as she pulled her mouth down to his and asked for what she truly wanted.

"You, Max. I want you inside me. Now."

His fingers shaking with the need of his body, he reached around the shower curtain and ripped open the condom packet. All he remembered were her hands learning his body, her lips demanding kiss after kiss. He happily obliged her exploration until he could take no more.

"Now, honey."

"Yes."

He picked her up and her legs wrapped around his hips as he eased himself inside. He held his breath for a moment, filling her, expanding her warm sheath to accommodate his desire. With his strong hands holding her securely between the tile wall and his body, he began to move inside her. Slowly, at first. A thrust, a kiss. A thrust, a nibble of her ear. His lips moved lower with each thrust and she arched her back, offering him her body. He closed his mouth over the proud peak of her breast, swirled his tongue around her pearled nipple and she gasped.

His body demanded faster, harder, and hers accepted, welcomed, blossomed with his need.

The one glitch came when he pressed a kiss to the

scar on her collarbone. Her fingers tried to push his lips away. "Don't," she whispered. "They're ugly."

But Max insisted on gently kissing each mark. "Every inch of you is beautiful to me."

And then the need became too great. The rhythm between their bodies synced and moved together. The water ran, the heat consumed him. And with a final thrust that blinded him to all but the crazy, inexplicable love he had for this woman, Max poured himself out inside her.

A few minutes later, after catching their breaths and another quick rinse in the cooling shower, Rosie turned off the water. He wrapped a towel around his waist and another around her, then lifted her into his arms and carried her to bed.

He shoved a pair of bed-hog dogs onto the floor and laid her down. Max climbed in beside her, pulled the covers up over them both. Spooning his damp, spent body next to hers, he pulled Rosie to his chest, buried his nose in the sweet scent of her hair, and they drifted off into a deep, healing sleep together.

Chapter Eleven

Max awoke to a dog licking his ear and an empty pillow beside him.

A brief moment of panic—that Rosie had somehow been taken from him while he slept, with that dreadful sense of finality he'd felt the morning Jimmy hadn't shown up for their fishing weekend—roused him completely. But the panic quickly ebbed when he smelled the coffee brewing in the kitchen and heard the strains of an orchestra playing softly from another part of the house. Rosie was fine. Just an early riser, eager to get a start on a new day. Hopefully, not a woman who was having regrets about the night before.

And then there was the poodle who'd taken such a shine to him. Pushing aside Trixie's tongue, Max sat up. She switched the licking to his hand until he spared a minute to give her a tummy rub. "Really? Is this going to be a thing with you?"

He set the fuzzy morning greeter on the floor and got up to use the bathroom, retrieving his shorts and jeans and pulling them on. He tucked his holster into the back of his belt and pulled out his phone to put in a quick call to Trent to get a status report.

"Morning, sunshine," Trent teased. "How'd you sleep?"

"Better than you, I'm guessin'. Anything I need to know about?"

"Everything's quiet out here. I got a call five minutes ago from Jim. He said Charleen Grimes left her condo, drove through a coffee shop, then went to work. Apparently, they're having a big summer clearance sale at her boutique if you're lookin' for a new dress."

"No, thanks." Max shook his head and went to the kitchen to pour himself a mug of coffee. Even after a stakeout, the younger detective was too chipper in the morning for his tastes. "Anything else?"

"You need to call Katie. She's got some information you'll want to hear."

"Got it. I've got my coffee now, so you can leave. Thanks for keeping an eye on things."

"Not a problem."

Max drank half his coffee and ate a cinnamon roll that he hoped Rosie had left out for him before dialing Katie's number.

"Good morning, Max." Was everyone he knew a morning person?

"Morning, kiddo. Trent said you had something for me?"

"You bet. I tracked down a short list of dark green, extended cab pickup trucks with black trim—sold in the KC area in the past month, so it would still have dealer stickers and not a registered license plate yet."

"How short is the list?"

"Three trucks. Here's where it gets interesting."

Normally he was amused by Katie's flair for drama, but this morning he just wanted to get the info and get back to Rosie. "Tell me, sunshine."

"All three were purchased as fleet vehicles for Endicott Global."

Max opened his mouth to swear but decided Katie didn't need to hear him any more than Rosie did. But that Wells woman had lied to them with a straight face. The CEO fit two of the three puzzle pieces—she had access to the drug that killed Richard Bratcher, and a company vehicle had been spotted near Rosie's house. "You did good, kiddo. Thanks."

More awake and on guard and ready to face whatever reaction Rosie had to that steamy shower they'd shared, he sought her out and found her sitting on the braided rug in the library. He needn't have worried about her having regrets or feeling self-conscious about her beautiful body or feeling pressured to turn one night into a full-blown relationship. She jumped up from the boxes and papers she'd been sorting and hurried across the room, smiling.

The jeans she wore kind of caught him off guard. He wouldn't have thought she even owned a pair with that wardrobe of dresses she usually wore. But he couldn't help but smile back—or cling to the kiss she rose up on tiptoe to give him. "Morning, Rosie Posy."

"Max, look what I found." She hadn't pinned her hair up yet, either, which distracted him from the stationery and envelopes she juggled in her hand. "I was going through some old letters Richard had written me. I felt like I was starting a new life today so I wanted to get rid of my past. I mean I'm thinking of myself as Rosie instead of Rosemary now. I'm not afraid some creep will come to my house every night anymore. I was going to throw away all these old letters he sent me."

He put a hand up to stop the philosophical discussion he wanted to hear more about—later—and urged her to get to the point. "What did you find, Rosie?"

"This." She tossed most of the letters she held into a box, then unfolded one stamped with the Bratcher law firm name at the top. A rock settled in Max's gut. This couldn't be good. "Richard must have stuck this letter in the wrong envelope. It's to his mistress, not me."

He took the letter. "You know, for a man I've never met, I sure do dislike him."

Rosie pointed to the salutation at the top of the paper. "Look who it's written to."

Max drew in a satisfied breath as the third piece of the puzzle fell into place.

Charleen Grimes wasn't the only woman Richard had cheated with.

"We've been looking for the wrong mistress."

It was a love letter to Hillary Wells.

"I'M TIRED OF WAITING."

"Sir, I told you she was on a conference call... Sir?"

Rosie nodded to the sputtering assistant at the front desk as Max flashed his badge and marched right past him into Hillary Wells's office at the Endicott Global building.

She plowed into Max's back when he suddenly stopped. He spun around to catch her hand and keep her from tumbling, but she could see what had stopped him. The office was empty.

"Is there a back door to this room?" Max asked. "She's not here."

The assistant stepped into the office and looked around, too. He threw up his hands as if surprised to see his boss had left.

Max clapped him on the shoulder and pushed him out of his path. "Nice stall, kid. You hear from the boss lady, tell her KCPD wants to have a conversation with her."

"Yes, sir."

While they were driving down the highway, Max

alerted the Cold Case Squad that Hillary Wells was in the wind. She'd skipped out on her appointment with Max and Rosie and hadn't left her contact information with her assistant. She wasn't answering any of her phones, and, according to Katie, who'd tried to locate her via GPS, Dr. Wells's cell phone had been turned off.

"Wait a minute." Katie hesitated, probably reading something off one of her computer screens. Rosie had put Max's cell on speaker and held it up for him to speak and hear while he drove the Chevelle.

"What is it, kiddo?" Max prompted.

"It looks like she has a cabin down by Truman Lake. I've got a ping off her vehicle's smart system there."

"Give me a twenty." Once Katie gave them the cabin's location and directions to get to it, Max made his way to the south end of the city and drove over to one of Missouri's most popular recreation areas.

An hour later, after a scenic drive through the northern edge of the Missouri Ozarks, they pulled into a gravel driveway behind a dark green pickup truck.

"Son of a gun." Katie's research was right on the money. "She's here," Max announced, nodding toward the windows along the front of the cabin that had been opened to let in the warm summer breeze. He took Rosie's hand and pulled her into step beside him and they walked to the front door. "Today, maybe you'd better let me do the talking. I have a feeling the good doctor won't be such a cooperative witness this time." He knocked on the door. "KCPD. It's Detective Krolikowski, Dr. Wells. I'd like to ask you a few more questions."

When the woman didn't immediately answer, Rosie asked, "How does this work, exactly—you ask her if she killed Richard?"

Max grinned. "Well, the direct approach doesn't usually work for most suspects."

"It worked for me."

He reached over and sifted his fingers through the ponytail hanging down the back of her T-shirt. "You, Rosie March, are the exception to most rules."

After more than a minute with no response, Max knocked again. "KCPD." He motioned Rosie to stand back to the side as he pulled his weapon.

His wary posture put her on guard, too. "Do you think something's wrong?"

His shoulders lifted with a deep breath. "I hope she hasn't done anything stupid like take some of her own drugs to get out of doing prison time."

"Suicide?"

Max's jaw trembled before he knocked on the door one last time. He was thinking of his friend Jimmy. "I'm comin' in, Dr. Wells."

Rosie clung to the safety of the wall while Max turned the knob and pushed open the door.

A gunshot exploded close to Rosie's ear and Max went flying back off the front step. "Max!"

He hit the ground with a horrible thud and pulled his knees up, groaning, rolling from side to side as the front of his shirt turned red with blood.

Hillary Wells marched out of the cabin, shifted the aim of her gun at Rosie and warned her, "Don't move."

Rosie clung to the cedar planking of the cabin while Hillary picked up Max's weapon, which had been jarred from his hand when he'd landed.

She unloaded the magazine of bullets from his gun and tossed the weapon one direction into the woods surrounding the house, and the magazine into the trees in the opposite direction.

Hillary turned back to Rosie, using her gun to give succinct directions. "Now handcuff his wrists together. Then get his keys and load him into the backseat of his car. You're driving."

ROSIE SWIPED AWAY the tears the spilled from the corner of her eye, not sure if they were tears of fear that Max's head kept lolling from one side to the other as he bled out into the backseat, or pure, white-hot anger for the woman sitting in the passenger seat, calmly giving driving directions while training her gun at Rosie to ensure her cooperation. She suspected it was a little of both. Hillary Wells had killed one man Rosie had thought she loved, and now the woman was going to kill Max. And that would be a loss from which Rosie was certain she'd never recover.

Rosie glanced down at the typed suicide note Hillary had forced her to sign by threatening to shoot Max again. The Endicott Global CEO had written an essay of pure fiction, where Rosie confessed to murdering her abusive ex-fiancé by filling a bottle of champagne with RUD-317, seducing him in his condo and sneaking out after he'd overdosed on the drug. When the Cold Case Squad detective unmasked her as the killer several years later, she shot him before her secret could be revealed. But she'd fallen in love with the detective and, regretting her rash action, killed herself.

Rosie shifted her grip on the wheel and tried to think of a way she could escape and get Max to an ER for medical treatment. He kept sliding in and out of consciousness. His breathing was labored and his skin was far too pale.

"No one who knows me will ever believe that note."

Hillary smirked. "They won't believe you're a strong enough woman to commit cold-blooded murder?"

"No. They won't believe I'd ever want to seduce Richard."

The deep-pitched chuckle from the backseat infused her with renewed strength and determination. "That's my girl," Max rasped.

But Hillary didn't appreciate the humor. "I knew you were going to be trouble. You couldn't be content, could you? Nobody could prove you murdered Richard, but as long as you were the police's prime suspect, no one was looking at me, either." She indicated a narrow side road and ordered Rosie to turn. "Richard was a scumbag—greedy, self-centered, violent—the world is better without him. It was a win-win situation. You weren't in jail and he was out of your life. But you had to know the truth, didn't you?"

"He's never been out of my life since I met him. Clearing my name is the only way I can finally say goodbye to his influence over me."

Sheer will seemed to fuel the grumbling voice from the backseat. "Why did you kill him, Doc? You didn't like that he cheated on you, too? Or are you just a man hater?"

"It was purely business." She pointed to a gravel road among the trees. "Turn here." Rosie obeyed, following Dr. Wells's directions deeper into the forested recreational area dotted with remote cabins around the dam and creeks that fed them. "Richard was a two-night stand. I picked him up in a hotel bar."

Rosie glanced in the rearview mirror. Max opened his eyes and nodded. He remembered it, too. Rosie had picked him up in a bar and recruited him into helping her. She hadn't regretted a moment of their time together since.

"How is murder a business deal?" Rosie asked, concentrating on the narrowing road. They were dropping in altitude, too. They were approaching a remote cove off the main lake.

"I needed someone else dead and out of my way before he cheated me out of my life's work and rightful position at the company."

"Lloyd Endicott?" Max guessed.

"Yes." The woman was completely unapologetic about the death of her so-called friend and mentor. "I knew I'd be the first person the police would look at if it was proved Lloyd's death was anything but accidental. So I made a deal with a colleague to arrange for his death, and in exchange, I was asked to eliminate Richard."

"Strangers on a Train," Max muttered.

"What?"

"Nothing. I have a couple of friends who like old movies."

Turning up her nose as if polite chitchat was beneath her, Hillary used the gun to give Rosie the next direction. "Pull up over there at the old boat ramp. Leave the engine running."

"Who wanted Richard dead?"

"I'm not allowed to say. A deal's a deal."

"Killing us can't be part of the deal. Isn't the trick to getting away with murder that you have an airtight alibi while someone else does the dirty work for you?"

"Hence, the signed confession. When your bodies are found, they'll find the letter and file your deaths away as a murder-suicide."

Rosie's heart squeezed in her chest at the pained

expression on Max's face. She knew it wasn't just the bullet hole in his gut, but the memory of his best friend's suicide that was tearing him up.

Forcing Max to suffer like this, taking away the man who'd given her a few days of happiness simply wasn't fair. Not after everything else she'd been through. She wasn't exactly sure what that feverish sensation flowing through her veins was, but Rosie was thinking that Max had been right about her. She wasn't that quiet, demure, fragile woman by nature—that was a persona she'd taken on to survive her life with Richard and the terrible years that followed. Rosie had a redheaded temper firing through her blood.

She shifted the Chevy into Park and looked straight ahead at the gray-green water and whitecaps below. "Dr. Wells, I think you should know that I would never commit suicide. I've fought too hard to survive and to find happiness. No one will believe the story. There'll be an investigation."

She found Max's questioning gaze in the mirror and darted her eyes twice to the right. *I've got a plan. It's a crazy one. But I'm not giving up without a fight.*

Max nodded. "Hooah." HUA.

Heard. Understood. Acknowledged.

Clutching his stomach, he sat up a little straighter. "I love you, Rosie."

"I love you."

"Isn't that just sickeningly sweet," Hillary sneered. "You know what to do. As soon as I get out, shift the car into Drive. I'll make your boyfriend's death as painless as possible—a shot to the head. Then you drive the car into the lake. Unless you'd rather me wait to put the gun in your hand after I shoot you, too?" The dark-haired woman laughed. "Personally, I'd choose drowning in this deep part of the lake. That way, at least, I'm giving you a sporting chance at surviving."

Rosie took a deep breath and shifted the car while Hillary unbuckled her safety belt and reached for the door handle. "I know you love this car, Sergeant."

His expression turned as grim as she'd ever seen it. "Do it!"

Rosie stomped on the accelerator as Hillary turned to shoot Max. The car jerked forward, toppling the woman off balance. When she tumbled back against the seat, Max surged forward with a feral roar, looping his handcuffs around Hillary's neck as the gun fired.

"Max!" She heard his grunt of pain, saw the red circle appear on his shoulder and stain the front of his shirt.

His stranglehold on Dr. Wells went slack. "What are you doing? Stop!" she cried, struggling to free herself from the noose of Max's arms.

There was nothing Rosie could do but hold on and pray as the Chevy leaped the top of the boat ramp and hit the old concrete and rocks farther down. The car bottomed out, threw its passengers up to the ceiling. The gun bounced out of Hillary's hand and skittered along the floorboards. The other woman screamed as the car hit the water and plunged, nose first, in a slow-motion dive to the bottom of the lake.

The bruising wrench of the seat belt stunning Rosie quickly gave way to panic as the gray-green water rushed in. She was ankle-deep in the cool water before her brain kicked in. She quickly unhooked her seat belt and climbed up onto her knees to help Max escape.

"Max?" No answer. "Sergeant, can you hear me?" she shouted in a firmer voice. When his groggy eyes blinked open, she softened her command. "Can you unhook your seat belt?" She unlooped his arms from the headrest where he'd caught Hillary, then scrambled over the seat when the water rushed over his lap and his bound hands made it impossible to find the release.

Rosie spared a brief glance for the woman who'd tried to kill them, but at some point of impact, Hillary had struck her head and she was floating, unconscious, off her seat. Worrying more about the man she wanted desperately to save, Rosie took a breath and sank below the water that was pouring over the seat to release Max. When he, too, started to float, she pushed his body up to the ceiling where there was still air. "Breathe, honey. Take a deep breath."

She took several breaths herself, filling her lungs as deeply as she could before the translucent water hit the corner of her mouth and she sputtered.

She tipped her mouth to the ceiling. "Let me do the work, okay? Just don't fight me. You saved me, and now I'm going to save you."

He nodded his understanding before his eyes closed and the water rushed over his head. After snatching one last breath from a pocket of air, Rosie dove beneath the water to unlock Max's door and push it open. The changing water pressure made the car sink faster, but sucked them both out of the car when she grabbed onto his shirt and pulled him with her.

Then it was a series of kicks, a pull of her arm and ignoring the panicked need to breathe before she broke the surface of the water. Refilling her lungs with reviving air, she pulled Max's heavy body onto her hip and held his head above water as best she could while she fought the wind-tossed waves and swam in a sidestroke to shore. She was near exhaustion by the time she reached a shallow enough depth that she could stand.

"Stay with me, Max," she urged, wiping the water from his face and hair and dragging him to shore.

She slipped a couple of times trying to push him up onto the dry ground between the rushes, grass and rocks. He was conscious, at least, thank God, because once he could get his legs beneath him, he helped push himself higher onto the bank. But then she lost her footing on the slick, mossy rocks and fell into the water again, swallowing a mouthful as she sank beneath the surface. When she pushed herself back up, a hand latched onto hers. Relief swept through her as she surfaced.

"Max…" Stunned, she would have fallen again, but the man who pulled her from the water didn't release his grip. "You."

When the young man with the glasses finally let go, she scrambled away, crawling over Max's legs and kneeling in front of him to provide some sort of protection for her wounded hero. The young man who'd taken her picture at the prison that day picked up the suit jacket he'd tossed into the grass.

"You do good work, Miss March," he said, shrugging into his jacket.

"Who are you?"

"A friend of a friend who's looking out for you." He turned his gaze out to the water where there weren't even bubbles left to show where the car had sunk. "Dr. Wells was becoming a bit of a problem for us."

Max's big hand grazed her knee and held on, comforting her as some of his strength returned. "You're Asher's man."

"No, Detective. I'm my own man." Without any more explanation than that, the mysterious Glasses Guy climbed the hill toward a black Chrysler parked at the top. "I already called 9-1-1. An ambulance is en route.

I surely hope you don't bleed to death, Detective." He climbed inside his car and started the engine. "Ma'am. I think you'll understand that I'd rather not be here when the police arrive."

And with that, he drove away.

Rosie heard sirens in the distance and started to stand. But Max pulled her back to her knees. "Come here."

Without regard for modesty, she pulled off her T-shirt and wadded it up to stanch his wounds.

He splayed his fingers on her bare stomach and grinned. "Honey, I'm afraid I can't help you with that right now. Maybe later?"

How could he joke and flirt when she was so afraid? "Max. You're bleeding. Maybe dying. I don't want to lose you."

"Come. Here." He grabbed her and pulled her down into the grass beside him. He pressed a kiss to her temple and rubbed his grizzled cheek against hers. The sirens were getting closer. Glasses Guy hadn't lied. Help was coming. "Are you okay? Are you hurt?"

"I'm fine. You're the one who got shot. Twice."

"I'm gonna live through both. I'm a tough guy, remember?"

"Damn it, Max—"

"Rosemary March. Did you just swear? You know I don't like hearing that from you," he teased. He pulled her in for a kiss that lasted until a groan of pain forced him to come up for air. "You get under my skin, Rosie."

"Like an itchy rash?" she teased, pushing the wadded T-shirt back into place over his stomach wound.

"Like an alarm clock finally waking me up to the life I'm supposed to have. With you." So when did the tough guy learn to speak such beautiful things? Tears stung her eyes again as she found a spot where she could hug him without causing any pain. "I know I'm not the guy you expected to want you like this, and I know you weren't the woman I was looking for. Hell, I wasn't even looking."

"Neither was I."

"But we found each other."

"We're good for each other."

"I'm not an easy man to live with. I come with a lot of emotional baggage."

"And I don't?"

"You can do better than me."

Rosie shook her head, smiling. "I can't do better than a good man who loves me. A man who encourages me to be myself and to be strong and who makes me feel safer and more loved than I have ever felt in my life."

"I do love you, Rosie."

"I love you, Max." They shared another kiss until she realized the ambulance and two sheriff's cars were pulling to a stop at the top of the boat ramp.

"What are we going to do about these feelings?" Max asked.

"What do you want to do?"

"Let's give the Dinkles something to talk about."

"You're moving in upstairs?"

"And opening all the windows."

Rosie smiled. "Oh, I hope we give them plenty to talk about."

* * * * *

Watch for the thrilling conclusion to Julie Miller's
THE PRECINCT: COLD CASE *miniseries,*
on sale in December 2015. Look for it wherever
Harlequin Intrigue books and ebooks are sold!

Read on for a sneak peek of
LONE RIDER
The next installment in
THE MONTANA HAMILTONS *series*
from New York Times *bestselling author*
B.J. Daniels.
When danger claims her, rescue comes from the one
man she least expects…

CHAPTER ONE

THE MOMENT JACE CALDER saw his sister's face, he feared the worst. His heart sank. Emily, his troubled little sister, had been doing so well since she'd gotten the job at the Sarah Hamilton Foundation in Big Timber, Montana.

"What's wrong?" he asked as he removed his Stetson, pulled up a chair at the Big Timber Java coffee shop and sat down across from her. Tossing his hat on the seat of an adjacent chair, he braced himself for bad news.

Emily blinked her big blue eyes. Even though she was closing in on twenty-five, he often caught glimpses of the girl she'd been. Her pixie cut, once a dark brown like his own hair, was dyed black. From thirteen on, she'd been piercing anything she could. At sixteen she'd begun getting tattoos and drinking. It wasn't until she'd turned seventeen that she'd run away, taken up with a thirty-year-old biker drug-dealer thief and ended up in jail for the first time.

But while Emily still had the tattoos and the piercings, she'd changed after the birth of her daughter, and after snagging this job with Bo Hamilton.

"What's wrong is Bo," his sister said. Bo had insisted her employees at the foundation call her by her first name. "Pretty cool for a boss, huh?" his sister had said at the time. He'd been surprised. That didn't sound like the woman he knew.

But who knew what was in Bo's head lately. Four months ago her mother, Sarah, who everyone believed dead the past twenty-two years, had suddenly shown up out of nowhere. According to what he'd read in the papers, Sarah had no memory of the past twenty-two years.

He'd been worried it would hurt the foundation named for her. Not to mention what a shock it must have been for Bo.

Emily leaned toward him and whispered, "Bo's... She's gone."

"Gone?"

"Before she left Friday, she told me that she would be back by ten this morning. She hasn't shown up, and no one knows where she is."

That *did* sound like the Bo Hamilton he knew. The thought of her kicked up that old ache inside him. He'd been glad when Emily had found a job and moved back to town with her baby girl. But he'd often wished her employer had been anyone but Bo Hamilton—the woman he'd once asked to marry him.

He'd spent the past five years avoiding Bo, which wasn't easy in a county as small as Sweet Grass. Crossing paths with her, even after five years, still hurt. It riled him in a way that only made him mad at himself for letting her get to him after all this time.

"What do you mean, *gone*?" he asked now.

Emily looked pained. "I probably shouldn't be telling you this—"

"Em," he said impatiently. She'd been doing so well at this job, and she'd really turned her life around. He couldn't bear the thought that Bo's disappearance might derail her second chance. Em's three-year-old daughter, Jodie, desperately needed her mom to stay on track.

Leaning closer again, she whispered, "Apparently there are funds missing from the foundation. An auditor's been going over all the records since Friday."

He sat back in surprise. No matter what he thought of Bo, he'd never imagined this. The woman was already rich. She wouldn't need to divert funds...

"And that's not the worst of it," Emily said. "I was told she's on a camping trip in the mountains."

"So, she isn't really gone."

Em waved a hand. "She took her camping gear, saddled up and left Saturday afternoon. Apparently she's the one who called the auditor, so she knew he would be finished and wanting to talk to her this morning!"

Jace considered this news. If Bo really were on the run with the money, wouldn't she take her passport and her SUV as far as the nearest airport? But why would she run at all? He doubted Bo had ever had a problem that her daddy, the senator, hadn't fixed for her. She'd always had a safety net. Unlike him.

He'd been on his own since eighteen. He'd been a senior in high school, struggling to pay the bills, hang on to the ranch and raise his wild kid sister after his parents had been killed in a small plane crash. He'd managed to save the ranch, but he hadn't been equipped to raise Emily and had made his share of mistakes.

A few months ago, his sister had got out of jail and gone to work for Bo. He'd been surprised she'd given Emily a chance. He'd had to readjust his opinion of Bo—but only a little. Now this.

"There has to be an explanation," he said, even though he knew firsthand that Bo often acted impulsively. She did whatever she wanted, damn the world. But now his little sister was part of that world. How could she leave Emily and the rest of the staff at the foundation to face this alone?

"I sure hope everything is all right," his sister said. "Bo is so sweet."

Sweet wasn't a word he would have used to describe her. Sexy in a cowgirl way, yes, since most of the time she dressed in jeans, boots and a Western shirt—all of which accented her very nice curves. Her long, sandy-blond hair was often pulled up in a ponytail or wrestled into a braid that hung over one shoulder. Since her wide green eyes didn't need makeup to give her that girl-next-door look, she seldom wore it.

"I can't believe she wouldn't show up. Something must have happened," Emily said loyally.

He couldn't help being skeptical based on Bo's history. But given Em's concern, he didn't want to add his own kindling to the fire.

"Jace, I just have this bad feeling. You're the best tracker in these parts. I know it's a lot to ask, but would you go find her?"

He almost laughed. Given the bad blood between him and Bo? "I'm the last person—"

"I'm really worried about her. I know she wouldn't run off."

Jace wished *he* knew that. "Look, if you're really that concerned, maybe you should call the sheriff. He can get search and rescue—"

"No," Emily cried. "No one knows what's going on over at the foundation. We have to keep this quiet. That's why you have to go."

He'd never been able to deny his little sister anything, but this was asking too much.

"Please, Jace."

He swore silently. Maybe he'd get lucky and Bo

would return before he even got saddled up. "If you're that worried…" He got to his feet and reached for his hat, telling himself it shouldn't take him long to find Bo if she'd gone up into the Crazies, as the Crazy Mountains were known locally. He'd grown up in those mountains. His father had been an avid hunter who'd taught him everything about mountain survival.

If Bo had gone rogue with the foundation's funds… He hated to think what that would do not only to Emily's job but also to her recovery. She idolized her boss. So did Josie, who was allowed the run of the foundation office.

But finding Bo was one thing. Bringing her back to face the music might be another. He started to say as much to Emily, but she cut him off.

"Oh, Jace, thank you so much. If anyone can find her, it's you."

He smiled at his sister as he set his Stetson firmly on his head and made her a promise. "I'll find Bo Hamilton and bring her back." One way or the other.

CHAPTER TWO

BO HAMILTON ROSE with the sun, packed up camp and saddled up as a squirrel chattered at her from a nearby pine tree. Overhead, high in the Crazy Mountains, Montana's big, cloudless early summer sky had turned a brilliant blue. The day was already warm. Before she'd left, she'd heard a storm was coming in, but she'd known she'd be out of the mountains long before it hit.

She'd had a devil of a time getting to sleep last night, and after tossing and turning for hours in her sleeping bag, she had finally fallen into a death-like sleep.

But this morning, she'd awakened ready to face whatever would be awaiting her tomorrow back at the office in town. Coming up here in the mountains had been the best thing she could have done. For months she'd been worried and confused as small amounts of money kept disappearing from the foundation.

Then last week, she'd realized that more than a hundred thousand dollars was gone. She'd been so shocked that she hadn't been able to breathe, let alone think. That's when she'd called in an independent auditor. She just hoped she could find out what had happened to the money before anyone got wind of it—especially her father, Senator Buckmaster Hamilton.

Her stomach roiled at the thought. He'd always been

so proud of her for taking over the reins of the foundation that bore her mother's name. All her father needed was another scandal. He was running for the presidency of the United States, something he'd dreamed of for years. Now his daughter was about to go to jail for embezzlement. She could only imagine his disappointment in her—not to mention what it might do to the foundation.

She loved the work the foundation did, helping small businesses in their community. Her father had been worried that she couldn't handle the responsibility. She'd been determined to show him he was wrong. And show herself, as well. She'd grown up a lot in the past five years, and running the foundation had given her a sense of purpose she'd badly needed.

That's why she was anxious to find out the results of the audit now that her head was clear. The mountains always did that for her. Breathing in the fresh air now, she swung up in the saddle, spurred her horse and headed down the trail toward the ranch. She'd camped only a couple of hours back into the mountain, so she still had plenty of time, she thought as she rode. The last thing she wanted was to be late to meet with the auditor.

She'd known for some time that there were... *discrepancies* in foundation funds. A part of her had hoped that it was merely a mistake—that someone would realize he or she had made an error—so she wouldn't have to confront anyone about the slip.

Bo knew how naive that was, but she couldn't bear to think that one of her employees was behind the theft. Yes, her employees were a ragtag bunch. There was Albert Drum, a seventy-two-year-young former banker who worked with the recipients of the foundation loans. Emily Calder, twenty-four, took care of the website, research, communication and marketing. The only other employee was forty-eight-year-old widow Norma Branstetter, who was in charge of fund-raising.

Employees and board members reviewed the applications that came in for financial help. But Bo was the one responsible for the money that came and went through the foundation.

Unfortunately, she trusted her employees so much that she often let them run the place, including dealing with the financial end of things. She hadn't been paying close enough attention. How else could there be unexplained expenditures?

Her father had warned her about the people she hired, saying she had to be careful. But she loved giving jobs to those who desperately needed another chance. Her employees had become a second family to her.

Just the thought that one of her employees might be responsible made her sick to her stomach. True, she was a sucker for a hard-luck story. But she trusted the people she'd hired. The thought brought tears to her eyes. They all tried so hard and were so appreciative of their jobs. She refused to believe any one of them would steal from the foundation.

So what had happened to the missing funds?

She hadn't ridden far when her horse nickered and raised his head as if sniffing the wind. Spurring him forward, she continued through the dense trees. The pine boughs sighed in the breeze, releasing the smells of early summer in the mountains she'd grown up with. She loved the Crazy Mountains. She loved them especially at this time of year. They rose from the valley into high snow-capped peaks, the awe-inspiring range running for miles to the north like a mountainous island in a sea of grassy plains.

What she appreciated most about the Crazies was that a person could get lost in them, she thought. A hunter had done just that last year.

She'd ridden down the ridge some distance, the sun moving across the sky over her head, before she caught the strong smell of smoke. This morning she'd put her campfire out using the creek water nearby. Too much of Montana burned every summer because of lightning storms and careless people, so she'd made sure her fire was extinguished before she'd left.

Now reining in, she spotted the source of the smoke. A small campfire burned below her in the dense trees of a protected gully. She stared down into the camp as smoke curled up. While it wasn't that unusual to stumble across a backpacker this deep in the Crazies, it *was* strange for a camp to be so far off the trail. Also, she didn't see anyone below her on the mountain near the fire. Had whoever camped there failed to put out the fire before leaving?

Bo hesitated, feeling torn because she didn't want to take the time to ride all the way down the mountain to the out-of-the-way camp. Nor did she want to ride into anyone's camp unless necessary.

But if the camper had failed to put out the fire, that was another story.

"Hello?" she called down the mountainside.

A hawk let out a cry overhead, momentarily startling her.

"Hello?" she called again, louder.

No answer. No sign of anyone in the camp.

Bo let out an aggravated sigh and spurred her horse. She had a long ride back and didn't need a detour. But she still had plenty of time if she hurried. As she made her way down into the ravine, she caught glimpses of the camp and the smoking campfire, but nothing else.

The hidden-away camp finally came into view below her. She could see that whoever had camped there hadn't made any effort at all to put out the fire. She looked for horseshoe tracks but saw only boot prints in the dust that led down to the camp.

A quiet seemed to fall over the mountainside. No hawk called out again from high above the trees. No squirrel chattered at her from a pine bough. Even the breeze seemed to have gone silent.

Bo felt a sudden chill as if the sun had gone down— an instant before the man appeared so suddenly from out of the dense darkness of the trees. He grabbed her, yanked her down from the saddle and clamped an arm around her as he shoved the dirty blade of a knife in her face.

"Well, look at you," he said hoarsely against her ear. "Ain't you a sight for sore eyes? Guess it's my lucky day."

JACE HAD JUST knocked at the door when another truck drove up from the direction of the corrals. As Senator Buckmaster Hamilton himself opened the door, he looked past Jace's shoulder. Jace glanced back to see Cooper Barnett climb out of his truck and walk toward them.

Jace turned back around. "I'm Jace Calder," he said, holding out his hand as the senator's gaze shifted to him.

The senator frowned but shook his hand. "I know who you are. I'm just wondering what's got you on my doorstep so early in the morning."

"I'm here about your daughter Bo."

Buckmaster looked to Cooper. "Tell me you aren't here about my daughter Olivia."

Cooper laughed. "My pregnant bride is just fine, thanks."

The senator let out an exaggerated breath and turned his attention back to Jace. "What's this about—" But before he could finish, a tall, elegant blonde woman appeared at his side. Jace recognized Angelina Broadwater Hamilton, the senator's second wife. The rumors about her being kicked out of the house to make way for Buckmaster's first wife weren't true, it seemed.

She put a hand on Buckmaster's arm. "It's the auditor calling from the foundation office. He's looking for Bo. She didn't show up for work today, and there seems to be a problem."

"That's why I'm here," Jace said.

"Me, too," Cooper said, sounding surprised.

"Come in, then," Buckmaster said, waving both men inside. Once he'd closed the big door behind them, he asked, "Now, what's this about Bo?"

"I was just talking to one of the wranglers," Cooper said, jumping in ahead of Jace. "Bo apparently left Saturday afternoon on horseback, saying she'd be back this morning, but she hasn't returned."

"That's what I heard, as well," Jace said, taking the opening. "I need to know where she might have gone."

Both Buckmaster and Cooper looked to him. "You sound as if you're planning to go after her," the senator said.

"I am."

"Why would you do that? I didn't think you two were seeing each other?" Cooper asked like the protective brother-in-law he was.

"We're not," Jace said.

"Wait a minute," the senator said. "You're the one who stood her up for the senior prom. I'll never forget it. My baby cried for weeks."

Jace nodded. "That would be me."

"But you've dated Bo more recently than senior prom," Buckmaster was saying.

"Five years ago," he said. "But that doesn't have anything to do with this. I have my reasons for wanting to see Bo come back. My sister works at the foundation."

"Why wouldn't Bo come back?" the senator demanded.

Behind him, Angelina made a disparaging sound. "Because there's money missing from the foundation along with your daughter." She looked at Jace. "You said your sister works down there?"

He smiled, seeing that she was clearly judgmental of the "kind of people" Bo had hired to work at the foundation. "My sister doesn't have access to any of the money, if that's what you're worried about." He turned to the senator again. "The auditor is down at the foundation office, trying to sort it out. Bo needs to be there. I thought you might have some idea where she might have gone in the mountains. I thought I'd go find her."

The senator looked to his son-in-law. Cooper shrugged.

"Cooper, you were told she planned to be back Sunday?" her father said. "She probably changed her mind or went too far, not realizing how long it would take her to get back. If she had an appointment today with an auditor, I'm sure she's on her way as we speak."

"Or she's hiding up there and doesn't want to be found," Angelina quipped from the couch. "If she took that money, she could be miles from here by now." She groaned. "It's always something with your girls, isn't it?"

"I highly doubt Bo has taken off with any foundation money," the senator said and shot his wife a disgruntled look. "Every minor problem isn't a major scandal," he said and sighed, clearly irritated with his wife.

When he and Bo had dated, she'd told him that her stepmother was always quick to blame her and her sisters no matter the situation. As far as Jace could tell, there was no love lost on either side.

"Maybe we should call the sheriff," Cooper said.

Angelina let out a cry. "That's all we need—more negative publicity. It will be bad enough when this gets out. But if search and rescue is called in and the sheriff has to go up there… For all we know, Bo could be meeting someone in those mountains."

Jace hadn't considered she might have an accomplice. "That's why I'm the best person to go after her."

"How do you figure that?" Cooper demanded, giving him a hard look.

"She already doesn't like me, and the feeling is mutual. Maybe you're right and she's hightailing it home as we speak," Jace said. "But whatever's going on with her, I'm going to find her and make sure she gets back."

"You sound pretty confident of that," the senator said sounding almost amused.

"I know these mountains, and I'm not a bad tracker. I'll find her. But that's big country. My search would go faster if I have some idea where she was headed when she left."

"There's a trail to the west of the ranch that connects with the Sweet Grass Creek trail," her father said.

Jace rubbed a hand over his jaw. "That trail forks not far up."

"She usually goes to the first camping spot before the fork," the senator said. "It's only a couple of hours back in. I'm sure she wouldn't go any farther than that. It's along Loco Creek."

"I know that spot," Jace said.

Cooper looked to his father-in-law. "You want me to get some men together and go search for her? That makes more sense than sending—"

Buckmaster shook his head and turned to Jace. "I remember your father. The two of you were volunteers on a search years ago. I was impressed with both of you. I'm putting my money on you finding her if she doesn't turn up on her own. I'll give you 'til sundown."

"Make it twenty-four hours. There's a storm coming so I plan to be back before it hits. If we're both not back by then, send in the cavalry," he said and with a tip of his hat, headed for the door.

Behind him, he heard Cooper say, "Sending him could be a mistake."

"The cowboy's mistake," Buckmaster said. "I know my daughter. She's on her way back, and she isn't going to like that young man tracking her down. Jace Calder is the one she almost married."

Find out what happens next in
LONE RIDER
by New York Times
bestselling author B.J. Daniels
available August 2015,
wherever HQN Books and ebooks are sold.
www.Harlequin.com